Eight Mortal Ladies Possessed

By TENNESSEE WILLIAMS

TENNESSEE WILLIAMS

Eight Mortal Ladies Possessed

A BOOK OF STORIES

A New Directions Book

ACKNOWLEDGMENTS
Grateful acknowledgment is made to the editors and publishers of books
and magazines in which some of the stories in this collection
previously appeared: to *Playboy*, for "The Inventory at Fontana Bella"
and "Miss Coynte of Greene"; to *Playgirl* for "Sabbatha and Solitude";
and to *Vogue*, for "Oriflamme." "Happy August the Tenth," first
published in *Antaeus* and reprinted in *Esquire*, was included in *Best
American Short Stories of 1973* (Houghton Mifflin Company),
edited by Martha Foley.

First published clothbound (ISBN: 0-8112-0530-4)
and as New Directions
Paperbook 374 (ISBN: 0-8112-0531-2) in 1974
Published simultaneously in Canada by McClelland & Stewart, Ltd.
Manufactured in the United States of America

New Directions Books are published for James Laughlin
by New Directions Publishing Corporation,
333 Sixth Avenue, New York 10014

SECOND PRINTING

CONTENTS

Eight Mortal Ladies Possessed

Happy August the Tenth

Happy August the Tenth

The day had begun unpleasantly at breakfast, in fact it had gotten off on a definitely wrong foot before breakfast when Horne had popped her head into the narrow "study" which served as Elphinstone's bedroom for that month and the next of summer, and she, Horne, had shrieked at her, Happy August the Tenth! and then had popped out again and slammed the door shut, ripping off Elphinstone's sleep which was at best a shallow and difficult sleep and which was sometimes practically no sleep at all.

The problem was that Horne, by long understanding between the two ladies, had the air-conditioned master bedroom for the months of August and September, Elphinstone having it the other months of the year. Superficially this would appear to be an arrangement which was more than equitable to Elphinstone. It had been amicably arranged between the ladies when they had taken occupancy of the apartment ten years ago, but things that have been amicably arranged that long ago may become onerous to one or the other of the consenting parties as time goes on and, looking back now at this arrangement between them, Elphinstone suspected that Horne, being a New Yorker born and bred, must have known that she was going to enjoy the air-conditioner during the really hot, hot part of the summer. In fact, if Elphinstone's recollection served her correctly, Horne had admitted that August was usually the hottest month in Manhattan and that September was rarely inclined to cool it, but she, Horne, had reminded Elphinstone that she had her mother's cool summer retreat, Shadow Glade, to visit whenever she wished and Horne had also reminded her that she did not have to waken early in summer or in any season, since she was self-employed, more or less, as a genealogical consultant, specializing in F.F.V.'s, while she, Horne, had to adhere to a rather strict office schedule.

During these ruminations, Elphinstone had gotten up and gone to the bathroom and was now about to appear with ominous dignity (she hoped) in the living room at the back of their little fifth-floor brownstone apartment on East Sixty-first Street. Elphinstone knew that she was not looking well for she had glanced at the mirror. Middle age was not approaching on stealthy little cat feet this summer but was bursting upon her as peremptorily as Horne had shrieked her into August the Tenth.

What is August the Tenth? she asked Horne in a deceptively casual tone as she came into the living room for coffee.

Horne chuckled and said, August the Tenth is just August the Tenth.

Then you had no reason at all to wake me up at this hour?

I woke you up early because you told me last night to wake you up as soon as I woke up because Doc Schreiber had switched your hour to nine o'clock today in order to observe your state of mind in the morning.

Well, he is not going to observe it this morning after my third consecutive night with no sleep.

You don't think he ought to observe your awful morning depression?

My morning depressions are related only to prolonged loss of sleep and not to any problems I'm working out with Schreiber, and I am not about to pay him a dollar a minute to occupy that couch when I'm too exhausted to speak a mumbling word to the man.

You might be able to catch a few extra winks on the couch, Horne suggested lightly. And you know, Elphinstone, I'm more

4

and more convinced that your chronic irritability which has gotten much worse this summer is an unconscious reaction to the Freudian insult. You are an Aries, dear, and Aries people, especially with Capricorn rising, can only benefit from Jung. I mean for Aries people it's practically Jung or nothing.

Elphinstone felt a retort of a fulminous nature boiling in her breast but she thought it best, in her exhausted state, to repress it, so she switched the subject to their Panamanian parrot, Lorita, having observed that Lorita was not in her indoor cage.

Where have you put Lorita? she demanded as sharply as if she suspected her friend of having wrung the bird's neck and thrown it into the garbage-disposal unit.

Lorita is on her travels, said Horne briskly.

I don't think Lorita ought to go on her travels till you have gone to your office, Elphinstone grumbled, since you move around so fast in the morning that you are likely to crush her underfoot.

I move rapidly but not blindly, dear, and anyhow Lorita's gone to sit in her summer palace.

Lorita's summer palace was a very spacious and fancy cage that had been set up for her on the little balcony outside the double French doors, and there she was, in it, sitting.

Someday, said Elphinstone darkly, that bird is going to discover that she can fly, and then good-by Lorita!

You're full of dire predictions this morning, said Horne. Old Doc Schreiber is going to catch an earful, I bet!

Both were now sipping their coffee, side by side on the little ivory-satin-covered love seat that faced the television and the balcony and the backs of brownstone buildings on East Sixtieth Street. It was a pleasant view with a great deal more foliage than you usually see in Manhattan outside the park. The TV was on. A public-health official was talking about the increased incidence of poliomyelitis in New York that summer.

When are you going for your polio shots? asked Horne.

5

Elphinstone declared that she had decided not to have the polio shots this summer.

Are you mad? asked Horne.

No, just over forty, said Elphinstone.

What's that got to do with it?

I'm out of the danger zone, Elphinstone boasted.

That's an exploded theory. The man just said that there is no real age limit for polio nowadays.

Horne, you will take any shot or pill in existence, Elphinstone said, but for a very odd reason. Not because you are really scared of illness or mortality, but because you have an unconscious death wish and feel so guilty about it that you are constantly trying to convince yourself that you are doing everything possible to improve your health and to prolong your life.

They were talking quietly but did not look at each other as they talked, which was not a good sign for August the Tenth nor for the flowers of friendship.

Yes, that *is* a "very odd reason," a very odd one, indeed! Why should I have a death wish?

Their voices had become low and shaky.

Yesterday evening, Horne, you looked out at the city from the balcony and you said, My God, what a lot of big tombstones, a necropolis with brilliant illumination, the biggest tombstones in the world's biggest necropolis. I repeated this remark to Dr. Schreiber and told him it had upset me terribly. He said, "You are living with, you are sharing your life with, a very sick person. To see great architecture in a great city and call it tombstones in a necropolis is a symptom of a deep psychic disturbance, deeper than yours, and though I know how much you value this companion, I have to warn you that this degree of nihilism and this death wish is not what you should be continually exposing yourself to, during this effort you're making to climb back out of the shadows. I can only encourage you to go on with this relationship provided that this sick person will take psychotherapy, too. But I doubt that she will do this, since she doesn't want to climb up, she wants to move in the opposite direction. And this," he said, "is made very clear by what you've told me about her present choice of associates."

There was a little silence between them, then Horne said: Do you believe that I am an obstacle to your analysis? Because if you do, I want to assure you that the obstacle will remove itself gladly.

Schreiber is chiefly concerned, said Elphinstone, about your new circle of friends because he feels they're instinctively destructive!

Well, said Horne, he hasn't met them and I think it's awfully presumptuous to judge any group of varied personalities without direct personal contact. Of course I have no idea what stories about my friends you may have fed Doc Schreiber.

None, none! —Hardly any. . . .

Then how does he know about them? By some sort of divination?

In deep analysis, said Elphinstone portentously, you have to hold nothing back.

But that doesn't mean that what you don't hold back is necessarily true. Does it? Shit, apparently you didn't mean a word of it when you told me you understood how I need to have my own little circle of friends since I'm not accepted by yours.

Elphinstone replied sorrowfully, I have no circle of friends unless you mean my group of old school chums from Sarah Lawrence whom I have lunch with once a month, and very, very occasionally entertain here for a buffet supper and bridge, occasions to which you're always invited, in fact urged to come, but you have declined, except for a single occasion.

Oh, yes, said Horne, you said a few days ago that you not only saw nothing wrong in our having our little separate circle of friends, but you said you thought it was psychologically healthy for us both. You said, if you'd try to remember, that it relieved the tensions between us for each to have her own little social circle, and as for my circle being hostile to you, I can only tell *you*—

Tell me *what*?

That *you* did not accept *them*, you bristled like a hedgehog on the one occasion you honored them with your presence, the single time that you condescended to meet them instead of running out to some dreary get-together of old Sarah Lawrence alumnae.

Another pause occurred in the conversation. Both of them made little noises in their throats and took little sips of coffee and didn't glance at each other: the warm air trembled between them. Even the parrot Lorita seemed to sense the domestic crisis and was making quiet clucking sounds and little musical whistles from her summer palace, as if to pacify the unhappy ladies.

You say I have a death wish, said Horne, resuming the talk between them. I think you are putting the shoe on the wrong foot, dear. My direction is outward toward widening and enriching my contacts with life, but you are obsessed with the slow death of your mother, as if you envied her for it. You hate what you call "my circle of Village hippies" because they're intellectually vital, intensely alive, and dedicated to living, in *here*, and in *here*, and in *here*.

(She touched her forehead, her chest, and her abdomen with her three heres.)

Oh, and all this remarkably diversified vitality is about to explode here again tonight, is it, Horne?

The social climate, said Horne, is likely to be somewhat more animated than you'll find things at Shadow Glade but then the only thing less animated than your mother's is the social climate at your Sarah Lawrence bashes. Elphinstone, why don't you skip this week end at your mother's and come to my little gathering here tonight and come with a different attitude than you brought to it before, I mean be sweet, natural, friendly, instead of charging the atmosphere with hostility and suspicion, and then I know they would understand you a little better and *you* would understand the excitement that I feel in contact with a group that has some kind of intellectual vitality going for them, and—

What you're implying is that Sarah Lawrence graduates are inevitably and exclusively dim-witted?

I wasn't thinking about Sarah Lawrence graduates, I am nothing to them and they are nothing to me. However, she continued, her voice gathering steam, I do feel it's somewhat ludicrous to make a religion, a fucking mystique, out of having once attended that snobbish institution of smugness!

Well, Horne, if you must know the truth, said Elphinstone, some of the ladies were a bit disconcerted by your lallocropia.

My *what?*

Lallocropia is the psychiatric term for a compulsion to use shocking language, even on the least suitable occasions.

Shit, if I shocked the ladies—

Horne stood up on this line, which was left incomplete because her movement was so abrupt that she spilled some coffee on the ivory-satin cover of the love seat.

Horne cried out wildly when this happened, releasing in her outcry an arsenal of tensions which had accumulated during this black beginning of August the Tenth, and, as if projected by the cry, she made like a bullet for the kitchen to grab a dish-cloth and wet it at the faucet; then rushed back in to massage the coffee-stained spot on the elegant love seat with the wet cloth.

Oh, said Elphinstone in a tone more sorrowful than rancorous, I see now why this piece of furniture has been destroyed. You rub this ivory-satin cover, made out of my grandmother's wedding gown, with a wet dishcloth whenever you spill something on it which you do with a very peculiar regularity because of hostility toward—

As a preliminary, yes! said Horne, having heard only the

9

beginning of Elphinstone's rueful indictment. Then, of course, I go over the spot with Miracle Cleanser.

What is Miracle Cleanser?

Miracle Cleanser, said Horne in several breathless gasps, her respiration disturbed by their tension and its explosion, is a marvelous product advertised by Johnny Carson on his "Tonight Show."

I see you are mad, said Elphinstone. Well, I am going to send out this sofa to be covered with coffee-colored burlap.

Of course there's not much I can do to protect my china and glassware from the havoc which I know is impending *ce soir!* The breakage of my Wedgwood and Haviland is a small price to pay for your cultural regeneration these past few months, if six months is a few! And I can't see into the future, but if this place isn't a shambles in—

Why don't you put your goddamn Wedgwood and your Haviland in storage, who wants or needs your goddamn—

Horne, said Elphinstone with a warning vibration in her voice.

Horne replied with that scatological syllable which she used so often in conversations lately, and Elphinstone repeated her friend's surname with even more emphasis.

Christ, Elphinstone, but I mean it. We are sharing a little apartment in which nearly all the space is pre-empted by family relics such as your Wedgwood and your crystal and your silver with your mother's crest on it, everything's mother's or mother's mother's mother's around here so that I feel like a squatter in your family plot in the boneyard, and oh, my God, the bookshelves! Imagine my embarrassment when doctors of letters and philosophy go up to check the books on those shelves and see nothing but all this genealogical crap and think it's my choice of reading matter, *Notable Southern Families Volume I*, *Notable Southern Families Volume II*, *Notable Southern Bullshit* up to the ceiling and down to your Aubusson carpet, shelves and shelves and—

Horne, I believe you know that I am a professional consultant in genealogy and must have my reference books and that I have to work in this room!

Shit, I thought you had it all in your head by this time! Who buggered Governor Dinwiddie in the cranberry bushes, by the Potomac, which tribe scalped Mistress Elphinstone, the Cherokees or the Choctaws, at the—

There's nothing to be ashamed of in a colonial heritage, Horne!

Well, your colonial heritage, Elphinstone, and your family relics have made this place untenable for me! I am going to check into the Chelsea Hotel for the week end and you'll hear from me later about where to contact me for a reimbursement of my half of the rent money on this Elphinstone sanctuary!

She heard Horne slam the door of the master bedroom and, pricking her ears, she could hear her defecting companion being very busy in there. There was much banging about for ten minutes or so before Horne left for her office and then Elphinstone got up off the ruined love seat and went into the master bedroom for a bit of reconnaissance. It was productive of something in the nature of reassurance. Elphinstone discovered that Horne had packed a few things in a helter-skelter fashion in her Val-pac, had broken the zipper on it, and had left out her toilet articles, even her toothbrush, and so Elphinstone was reasonably certain the half-packed Val-pac was only one of Horne's little childish gestures.

At noon of August the Tenth, Elphinstone phoned the research department of the *National Journal of Social Commentary* which employed Horne and she got Horne on the phone.

Both voices were sad and subdued, so subdued that each had to ask the other to repeat certain things that were said in the long and hesitant phone conversation between them. The conversation was gentle and almost elegiac in tone. Only one controversial topic was brought up, the matter of the polio shots. Elphinstone said, Dear, if it will make you feel better, I'll go for

11

a polio shot. There was a slight pause and a catch in Horne's voice when she replied to this offer.

Dear, she said, you know the horror I have of poliomyelitis since it struck my first cousin Alfie who is still in the iron lung, just his head sticking out, wasted like a death's head, dear, and his lost blue eyes, oh, my God, the look in them when he tries to smile at me, oh, my God, that look!

Both of them started to weep at this point in the conversation and were barely able to utter audible good-bys. . . .

But at four o'clock that hot August afternoon there was a sudden change in Elphinstone's mood. Having made an afternoon appointment with her analyst, she recounted with marvelous accuracy the whole morning talk with Horne.

When will you learn, he asked sadly, when a thing is washed up?

He rose from his chair behind the couch on which Elphinstone was stretched, holding a wad of Kleenex to her nostrils; he was terminating the session after only twenty-five minutes of it, thus cheating Elphinstone out of half she paid for it.

Gravely he held the door open for Elphinstone to go forth. She went sobbing into the hot afternoon. It was overcast but blazing.

Nothing, nothing, she thought. She meant she had nothing to do. But when she went home, an aggressive impulse seized her. She went into the master bedroom and completed Horne's packing, very thoroughly, very quickly and neatly, and placed all four pieces of luggage by the bedroom door. Then she went to her own room, packed a zipper bag of week end things, and cut out to Grand Central Station, taking a train to Shadow Glade where she intended to stay till Horne had taken the radical hint and evacuated the East Sixty-first Street premises for good.

When she arrived at Mama's, Elphinstone found her suffering again from cardiac asthma, having another crisis with a nurse in attendance. She could feel nothing about it, except the usual shameful speculation about Mama's last will and testament: would the estate go mostly to the married sister with three children or had Mama been fair about it and realized that Elphinstone was really the one who needed financial protection over the years to come, or would it all go (oh, God) to the Knowledgist Church and its missionary efforts in New Zealand, which had been Mama's pet interest in recent years. Elphinstone was sickened by this base consideration in her heart, and when Mama's attack of cardiac asthma subsided and Mama got out of bed and began to talk about the Knowledgist faith again, Elphinstone was relieved, and she suddenly told Mama that she thought she, Elphinstone, had better go back to New York, since she had left without letting Horne know that she was leaving, which was not a kind thing to do to such a nervous person as Horne.

I don't understand this everlasting business of Horne, Horne, complained Mama. What the devil is Horne? I've heard nothing but Horne out of you for ten years running. Doesn't this Horne have a Christian name to be called by you? Oh, my God, there's something peculiar about it, I've always thought so. What's it *mean?* I don't know what to imagine!

Oh, Mama, there's nothing for you to imagine, said Elphinstone. We are two unmarried professional women and unmarried professional women address each other by surnames. It's a professional woman's practice in Manhattan, that's all there is to it, Mama.

Oh, said Mama, hmmm, I don't know, well. . . .

She gave Elphinstone a little darting glance but dropped the subject of Horne and asked the nurse in attendance to help her onto the potty.

Well, the old lady had pulled through another very serious attack of cardiac asthma and was now inclined to be comforted by little ministrations and also by the successful cheese soufflé which Elphinstone had prepared for their bedside supper.

13

Then Mama was further comforted and reassured by the doctor's dismissal of the nurse in attendance.

The doctor must think I'm better, she observed to her daughter.

Elphinstone said, Yes, Mama, your face was blue when I got here but now it's almost returned to a normal color.

Blue? said Mama.

Yes, Mama, almost purple. It's a condition called cyanosis.

Oh, my God, Mama sighed, cyna—*what* did you call it?

Observing that her use of such clinical terminology had upset Mama again, Elphinstone made a number of more conventional remarks such as how becoming Mama's little pink bed jacket looked on her now that her face had returned to a normal shade, and she reminded Mama that she had given Mama this bed jacket along with a pair of knitted booties and an embroidered cover for the hot-water bottle on Mama's eighty-fifth birthday.

After a little silence she could not suppress the spoken recollection that Mama's other daughter, the married one, Violet, had completely ignored Mama's birthday, as had the grandchildren Charlie and Clem and Eunice.

But Mama was no longer attentive, her sedation had begun to work on her now, and the slow and comparatively placid rise and fall of her huge old bosom suggested to Elphinstone the swells and lapses of an ocean that was subsiding from the violence of a typhoon.

It's wonderful how she keeps fighting off Mr. Black, said Elphinstone to herself. (Mr. Black was her private name for The Reaper.)

Lacey, said Elphinstone to her Mama's housekeeper, has Mama received any visits from her lawyer lately?

The old housekeeper had prepared a toddy of hot buttered rum for Elphinstone and given her the schedule of morning trains to Manhattan.

14

Sipping the toddy, Elphinstone felt reassured about Mama's old housekeeper. She'd sometimes suspected Lacey of having a sly intention of surviving Mama and so receiving some portion of Mama's estate, but now, this midnight, it was clearly apparent to Elphinstone that the ancient housekeeper was really unlikely to last as long as Mama. She had asthma, too, as well as rheumatoid arthritis with calcium deposits in the spine so that she walked bent over like a bow, in fact her physical condition struck Elphinstone as being worse than Mama's although she, Lacey, continued to work and move around with it, having that sort of animal tenacity to the habit of existence which Elphinstone was not quite certain that she respected either in Mama or in Mama's old housekeeper.

She can't hang on forever, Elphinstone murmured, half aloud.

What's that, Miss? inquired the housekeeper.

I said that Mama is still obsessed with the Knowledgist Church in spite of the fact it never got out of New Zealand where it originated a year before Mama's conversion, on her visit to Auckland with Papa when he failed to recuperate from the removal of his prostate in 1912....

What?

Nothing, she replied gently to the housekeeper's question. Then she raised her voice and said, *Will you please call me a cab now?*

What?

Cab! Call! Now!

Oh....

Yes, I've decided not to wait for the morning train to Manhattan but to return in a taxi. It will be expensive, but—

The sentence, uncompleted, would have been, if completed, to the effect that she intended to surprise Horne in the midst of a Babylonian revel with her N.Y.U. crowd, and she was thinking particularly of a remark she would make to the red-bearded philosophy prof.

Are you an advocate of women's lib, she would ask, for strictly personal reasons?

A slow smile grew on her face as she descended the stairs to the entrance hall of Mama's summer haven.

Hmmm, she reflected.

Her mood was so much improved by her masterly stratagem that she slipped a dollar bill into Lacey's old lizard-chill fingers at the door.

The cab was there.

Told that the fare to Manhattan would probably amount to about eighty dollars, Elphinstone angrily dismissed the driver, but before he had turned onto the highway from the drive she called him back in a voice like a clap of thunder.

It had occurred to Elphinstone that eighty dollars was less than half the cost of two sessions with Schreiber and she suspected so strongly that she was nearly certain that on the early morning of August the Eleventh her little home would be exorcised forever of the demonology and other mischiefs related to that circle from N.Y.U. as well as—

Yes, Horne will attempt to stick to me like a tar baby, but we'll see about that!

When Elphinstone admitted herself by latchkey to the Sixty-first Street apartment, she was confronted by a scene far different from that which she had anticipated all of the long and costly way home.

No revel was in progress, no sign of disorder was to be seen in the Horne-Elphinstone establishment.

Horne? Where *is* she? Oh, there!

Horne was seated in sleep on the ruinously stained love seat. She was facing the idiot box. It was still turned on, although it was after "The Tonight Show" had been wrapped up and even the "Late-Late Movie." The screen was just a crazy white blaze of light with little swirling black dots on it, it was like a negative film clip of a blizzard in some desolate country and it was accompanied, soundwise, by a subdued static roar. Why, my God, it was just like the conscious and unconscious mental processes of Elphinstone were being played back aloud from a sound track made silently during that prodigal gesture of a cab ride home, Christ Jesus.

Elphinstone studied the small, drooping figure of Horne asleep on the love seat, Horne's soft snoring interspersed with her unintelligible murmurs. Before her, on the little cocktail table, was half a bottle of Jack Daniel's Black Label and a single tumbler.

Apparently Horne had drunk herself to sleep in front of that idiot box, quite, quite alone. . . .

Elphinstone was in the presence of a mystery.

She checked with their answering service, requesting all messages for herself and Horne, too.

The single one which she had received was from a Sarah Lawrence graduate who was canceling a luncheon appointment because of a touch of the flu. The single message for Horne was more interesting. It said, with a brevity that struck Elphinstone as insulting, Sorry, no show, Sandy Cutsoe.

(The name was that of the red-bearded philosophy prof from the poison-ivy-league school.)

Sympathy for the small and abandoned person on the love seat entered Elphinstone's heart like the warm, peaceful drunkenness that comes from wine. She turned off the TV set, that negative film clip of a snowstorm at night in some way-off empty country, and then it was quite dark in the room and it was silent except for Horne's soft snores and murmurings and the occasional sleepy clucks of the parrot, still in her summer palace on the balcony where she might as well stay the night through.

Ah me, said Elphinstone, we've gotten through August the Tenth, that much is for sure anyhow. . . .

She did, then, a curious thing, a thing which she would

17

remember with embarrassment and would report to Schreiber on Monday in hope of obtaining some insight into the deeper meanings that it must surely contain.

She crouched before the love seat and gently pressed a cheek to Horne's bony kneecaps and encircled her thin calves with an arm. In this position, not comfortable but comforting, she watched the city's profile creep with understandable reluctance into morning, because, my God, yes, Horne's comment did fit those monolithic structures downtown, they truly were like a lot of illuminated tombstones in a necropolis.

The morning light did not seem to care for the city, it seemed to be creeping into it and around it with understandable aversion. The city and the morning were embracing each other as if they'd been hired to perform an act of intimacy that was equally abhorrent to them both.

Elphinstone whispered Happy August the Eleventh to Horne's kneecaps in a tone of condolence, and the day after tomorrow, no, after today, on Monday, she would begin her polio shots despite her childish dread of the prick of a needle.

August 1970

The Inventory at Fontana Bella

The Inventory at Fontana Bella

In the early autumn of her one hundred and second year the Principessa Lisabetta von Hohenzalt-Casalinghi was no longer able to tell light from dark, thunder from a footfall nor the texture of wool from satin. Yet she still got about with amazing agility. She danced to imaginary schottisches, polkas and waltzes with imaginary partners. She gave commands to household domestics in a voice whose volume would shame a drill sergeant. Having once been drawn through Oriental streets in rickshas, she had naturally learnt to yell "Chop, chop!" and she now exercised that command to make haste at the end of each order she shouted and these orders were given all but continually while she was awake and sometimes she would even shout "Chop, chop!" in her sleep.

Early in October, close to midnight, the Principessa sat bolt upright in her bed, breaking out of sleep as a sailfish from water.

"Sebastiano!" she cried, at the same instant of the cry pressing a hard fist to her groin.

Sebastiano was the name of her fifth and last husband who had now been dead for fifty years, and she had clutched her groin because in her dream she had felt the ecstasy of his penetration, a thing which had remained in her recollection more obsessively even than her commands to make haste.

Immediately after the outcry "Sebastiano," she slammed her fist down again, not on her nostalgic groin but upon the electric buttons that were on her bedside table, all eight of them were slammed down by her fist, hard and repeatedly and with continual cries of "Chop, chop!"

It was her resident physician who first responded, thinking that she had finally been stricken by a cardiac seizure.

"*Cristo*, no, this creature is immortal!" he shouted involuntarily as he entered Lisabetta's huge bedchamber and observed her standing naked by the bed in a state of existence that seemed to be nuclear powered, her blind eyes blazing with preternatural light.

In a number of minutes others assembled and were equally astounded by this phenomenon of vitality in so ancient a being.

"Preparations at once, chop chop. Fastest boat, *motoscafo* with the Rolls engine for lake crossing to Fontana Bella! Party including as follows. *Senta!* Secretaries, business and personal, upstairs and downstairs maids, especially Mariella who remembers Fontana Bella as well as I do. Lawyer, of course, not the old one gone blind but the young one with long beard that speaks High German, the curator of my museum, and of course my bookkeeper because the purpose of this trip is to finally hold, to conduct, an inventory of treasures at Fontana Bella, assessment of treasures remaining there, priceless art-objects and ancestral paintings, all, all valuables kept there, so get to it, chop, chop, teeth in, clothes on, off to Fontana Bella."

The crossing was not so tedious as most of the party had anticipated. The lawyer was soon engaged in the defloration of a very young chambermaid, first with his fingers and then with his tongue and, climactically, with his organ of gender, and the chambermaid's moans and cries were finally heard and mistaken by the Principessa for a noisy sea gull flying over the boat and she ordered it shot down at once. This provoked considerable merriment among the passengers: and then the curator of the Principessa's private gallery, brought along to assess the canvases at Fontana Bella, began to tell a story about a rather well-known and gifted Roman painter who had been recently transferred to an insane asylum in Zurich.

"Dear Florio," said the curator, "he could only set to work under very peculiar conditions. He had to have a barely pubescent youth in his studio. No, no, not as a model, no, not that, just as a sort of excitant to his creative juices, you see, but what's so amusing about it is that this nubile youth, picked up on the Spanish Steps by Florio's secretary, always had to be discovered naked in an alcove of the studio, a curtained alcove, with a peacock's feather inserted in his rectum, oh, no, not all the way in, just in far enough to hold it in place, and the alcove was kept curtained until Florio was seated at his easel. And then the curtain of the alcove would be drawn open by the secretary and he and Florio would utter ecstatic cries at the sight of the boy with the peacock's gorgeous tail feather up his bum and Florio then would cry out, *Ah, che bella sorpresa, uno pavone in casa mio!*"

(Which meant, What a lovely surprise, a peacock in my house!)

Then the boy would be paid nicely and dismissed from the house and Florio would start to paint like the madman he was.

At this story, there was general laughter loud enough to be heard by Lisabetta.

"*Silenzio*," she shouted and began to strike about her with her parasol. She managed to hit only the head of her poodle and when it barked at her in protest, she said: "You flatter me, sir, but we must wait upon another occasion!"

Then she fell asleep.

When the Principessa woke, she was in bed at Fontana Bella and it was again midnight.

She sprang up and shouted into a closet door, "Mariella, dress me, I want on woolens this morning, this is the north shore of Lago Maggiore, not the south, and there's no more disgusting affliction than a summer cold in the head. *Subito*, get them all up, the inventory is going to commence at once!"

Then she stood in the center of the bedroom, lifting legs to step into imaginary woolens and extending arms for the fur jacket which she thought was being put on her. She was quite impatient as the imaginary maid, Mariella, who had been dead for twenty years or more, did not seem to be following instructions with sufficient rapidity.

"Mariella," she shouted. "Teeth in, teeth in! Chop, chop!"

She opened her mouth for the dentures to be inserted.

"Hah, ring a bell, now *andiamo!*"

She then started across the great chamber, knocking over a couple of chairs which she mistook for assistant maids who were slow to get out of her way, and by an act of providence she walked straight to the door upon the hall.

The upper floor of Fontana Bella was still remarkably clear in her head since it was the floor on which she had lain with her great love, Sebastiano. She found the top of the grand staircase as if she had full possession of her sight and she descended it without a false step, at one point crying out, "Hands off me, I can't stand to be touched by anyone but a lover!"

The lower floor of Fontana Bella was more distinct in her mind than any part of her residence on the southern shore of Lago Maggiore and yet it was not as certain as she assumed it to be and at the foot of the stairs she made a wrong turn which brought her outdoors upon an enormous balustraded terrace that faced the gloomy lake that starless midnight.

"*Tutte qui?* All present for inventory? Chop, chop!"

Old ladies have a way, you know, of acquiring prejudice of race and class and gender, so it wasn't surprising that Lisabetta had turned somewhat against members of the Hebrew race, mostly through a paranoid senility.

"If there's a Jew at the inventory," she shouted, "I want him to keep a shut mouth. Not a word out of him during the inventory. I know they're an ancient race but not all ancient races are necessarily noble!"

This struck her as a witty observation and she gave forth a great peal of laughter to which some storks at a far end of the terrace responded with squawks and wing-flapping which Lisabetta interpreted as a flight of Jews from her presence.

"Gone, good! Proceed with the inventory, chop, chop! Oh, Christ, oh, wait, I have to relieve my bowels, put two screens about me and bring me a pot! Chop chop!"

She lowered herself to a squatting position until the windy disturbance in her bowels had subsided and then she stood up and remarked, "These things do happen, you know. It's a natural occurrence when there's so much agitation.

"Doctor, Doctor? Please examine my stool, each morning's stool ought to be examined, it's the key to existence. Now, then, that's over, on with the inventory!"

Lisabetta felt herself surrounded by the party which had accompanied her from the southern shore, that is, all but the possible Jews she'd ordered away.

"Ready? Ready? *Va bene!*"

She began to conduct the inventory, now, and it continued for seven hours. Her memory of her possessions at Fontana Bella was quite remarkable, as remarkable as her endurance.

It was an hour before daybreak when her truant party of attendants returned from the nearby casino but the Principessa was still on the terrace, pacing up and down it, naked in the gray moonlight. From a distance they heard her shouting, "Gold plate, service for eight! In the vault, yes, get the keys! Has the Jew made off with the keys? What, what? Don't shout, I cannot put up with this rushing about and shouting, hands off, I've told you and told you that I abhor the touch of anyone but a lover! You, you there, come here and explain something to me!"

She seemed to be pointing at the Neapolitan lawyer who was the first to approach her on the terrace, the rest standing back in attitudes of indifference and fatigue.

The lawyer was lively as ever. He went up close to the Principessa and shouted directly into her relatively good ear, "*Che vuolete, cara?*"

The old lady wheeled about to strike at him and the motion made her dizzy. She became disoriented but she was swift as ever as she rushed to the end of the terrace above which the storks were nesting, their patience exhausted by the disturbance beneath them. A great white female stork, alarmed for the safety of her young ones, flapped down from the roof onto Lisabetta to engage her in combat. It dove repeatedly at her head and her breast and abdomen, inflicting wounds with its beak and blows with its wings till the old lady toppled over and fell on the terrace pavement. Her naked and withered arms made frantic attempts to embrace the matron stork. At last she caught hold of its beak and would not let go. She divided her limbs and finally, she forced the stork's beak to penetrate her vagina. It stabbed and stabbed at her uterine passage, and still she kept calling out "Sebastiano" in a loud voice and "*Amore*" in a soft voice.

The lawyer caught hold of the stork's legs and tore it away from the lady. He held the bird up and announced, "The stork is dead, suffocated inside her, and still she's calling it lover!"

It was not voluntarily, nor even wittingly, that the Principessa returned across the lake the following day. The Neapolitan lawyer invented a story to entice the lady away from Fontana Bella: he told her that the owner of the nearby casino had arranged that evening a great gala in honor of her return to the province.

"All the walls of the gaming room are covered with talisman roses," the lawyer told her, "and your name is spelled out in camellias above the grand entrance."

When finally this invention had gotten through her left eardrum it did not surprise Lisabetta at all.

"Ah, well, I'll make an appearance, I suppose it is a case of *noblesse oblige.*"

The party got her seated among cushions in the stern of the *motoscafa* informing her it was a Mercedes limousine, and so the return voyage began.

The lake surface that day was smooth as glass and the sky was radiant.

"Perhaps a few turns of the wheel and some rolls of the dice, then home, chop chop, to continue the inventory. So many valuables are still not accounted for, and then, of course, you know—Mariella, cologne!"

A chambermaid passed a handkerchief to her. After a few sniffs of it, she resumed her talk, which seemed now to have gone into the babblings of delirium.

"If the moon were not clouded over, even if some stars were out, you would see behind Fontana Bella a bare hill with a bare tree on it. It ceased to leaf and to blossom when my last lover died."

That preface to her narrative was accurate in regard to the presence of the bare tree on the bare hill behind the villa.

"Sebastiano died as his name-saint died," she continued. "He was chained to a tree and his incomparable young body was transfixed by five arrows. I had five brothers, you know, one for each arrow that pierced him. They're dead now, I trust. No complaints, no demands from them lately. A family and a lover should never meet when a huge fortune's involved and questions of its division are involved, too, since there is no limit at all to the fantasies of hatred when great wealth is involved. First they tried to get His Holiness to annul my marriage to Sebastiano. Got nowhere with that and so resorted to arrows and, well, that was that. For them, emigration. For me a period in a convent. Oh, I tell you I have been a few places and I have done a few things and while I was in that convent I learned there are uses for candles beside the illumination of chapel altar and supper table, but it was *faute de mieux*, as the frogs put it, don't they?"

27

She fell into silent musing for a few moments: then, after a slight, bitter laugh, she spoke again.

"All good doctors," she said, "have telephone numbers that contain no more than one or two digits and the rest is all zeros, you know."

"Yes, and all good morticians," observed the lawyer, "have telephone numbers consisting of nothing but zero, zero, ad infinitum."

The curator of the museum was asked if he recalled any more amusing anecdotes about that Roman painter now confined to the asylum in Zurich.

"Well, yes, now, the last time I visited poor Florio, he seemed to have recovered completely. He kept assuring me that his aberrations were all gone under the excellent treatment at the retreat and he begged me to get his relatives in Rome to have him released, and I, being convinced that he really was quite well, embraced him and started for the gate and I had almost reached it when I was struck on the back of the head by a large piece of concrete paving that almost gave me a concussion but I managed to turn about and there was Florio behind me. And he had quite obviously thrown the missile. 'Don't forget now,' he shouted, 'I'm the sanest man in the world!' "

The passengers were laughing at this tale when Lisabetta leaned abruptly forward from her mound of pillows.

"Ah!"

With this exclamation, she struck a fist to her groin as if unbearably pained there but on the reptilian face of the Principessa was a look of ecstasy that outshone the glassy lake surface on that brightest of autumn mornings.

The Neapolitan lawyer, seated nearest her in the boat, seized her wrist and then, discovering no pulse, turned to the party and said, "A miracle has happened, the lady is dead."

This announcement caused one or two of the passengers to

cross themselves, perhaps while reflecting upon the difficulty of seeking new employment, but, understandably, most of the others in the boat were moved to much less solemn expressions of feeling.

July 1972

Miss Coynte of Greene

Miss Coynte of Greene

Miss Coynte of Greene was the unhappily dutiful caretaker of a bed-ridden grandmother. This old lady, the grandmother whom Miss Coynte addressed as *Mère* and sometimes secretly as *merde*, had outlived all relatives except Miss Coynte, who was a single lady approaching thirty.

The precise cause of Miss Coynte's grandmother's bed-ridden condition had never been satisfactorily explained to Miss Coynte by their physician in Greene, and Miss Coynte, though not particularly inclined to paranoia, entertained the suspicion that the old lady was simply too lazy to get herself up, even to enter the bathroom.

"What is the matter with *Mère*, Dr. Settle?"

"Matter with your grandmother?" he would say reflectively, looking into the middle distance. "Well, frankly, you know, I have not exactly determined anything of an organic nature that really accounts for her staying so much in bed."

"Dr. Settle, she does not stay so much in bed, but she stays constantly in it, if you know what I mean."

"Oh, yes, I know what you mean. . . ."

"Do you know, Dr. Settle, that I mean she is what they call 'incontinent' now, and that I have to spend half my time changing the linen on the bed?"

Dr. Settle was not unsettled at all by this report.

"It's one of a number of geriatric problems that one has to accept," he observed dreamily as he made toward the downstairs door. "Oh, where did I put my hat?"

"You didn't have one," replied Miss Coynte rather sharply.

He gave her a brief, somewhat suspicious glance, and said, "Well, possibly I left it in the office."

"Yes, possibly you left your head there, too."

"What was that you said?" inquired the old doctor, who had heard her perfectly well.

"I said that Chicken Little says the sky is falling," replied Miss Coynte without a change of expression.

The doctor nodded vaguely, gave her his practiced little smile and let himself out the door.

Miss Coynte's grandmother had two major articles on her bedside table. One of them was a telephone into which she babbled all but incessantly to anyone she remembered who was still living and of a social echelon that she regarded as speakable to, and the other important article was a loud-mouthed bell that she would ring between phone talks to summon Miss Coynte for some service.

Most frequently she would declare that the bed needed changing, and while Miss Coynte performed this odious service, *Mère* would often report the salient points of her latest phone conversation.

Rarely was there much in these reports that would be of interest to Miss Coynte, but now, on the day when this narrative begins, *Mère* engaged her granddaughter's attention with a lively but deadly little anecdote.

"You know, I was just talking to Susie and Susie told me that Dotty Reagan, you know Dotty Reagan, she weighs close to three hundred pounds, the fattest woman in Greene, and she goes everywhere with this peculiar little young man who they say is a fairy, if you know what I mean."

"No, *Mère*, can you swing over a little so I can change the sheet?"

"Well, anyway, Dotty Reagan was walking along the street

with this little fairy who hardly weighs ninety pounds, a breeze would blow him away, and they had reached the drugstore corner, where they were going to buy sodas, when Dotty Reagan said to the fairy, 'Catch me, I'm going to fall,' and the little fairy said to her, 'Dotty, you're too big to catch,' and so he let her fall on the drugstore corner."

"Oh," said Miss Coynte, still trying to tug the soiled sheet from under her grandmother's massive and immobile body on the brass bed.

"Yes, he let her fall. He made no effort to catch her."

"Oh," said Miss Coynte again.

"Is that all you can say, just 'Oh'?" inquired her grand-mother.

Miss Coynte had now managed by almost superhuman effort to get the soiled bed sheet from under her grandmother's great swollen body.

"No, I was going to ask you if anything was broken, I mean like a hipbone, when Dotty Reagan fell."

A slow and malicious smile began to appear on the face of Miss Coynte's grandmother.

"The coroner didn't examine the body for broken bones," the grandmother said, "since Dotty Reagan was stone-cold dead by the time she hit the pavement of the corner by the drugstore where she had intended to have an ice-cream soda with her fairy escort who didn't try to catch her when she told him that she was about to fall."

Miss Coynte did not smile at the humor of this story, for, despite her condition, an erotic, not a frigid, spinster approach-ing thirty, she had not acquired the malice of her grandmother, and, actually, she felt a sympathy both for the defunct Dotty Reagan and for the ninety-pound fairy who had declined to catch her.

"Were you listening to me or was I just wasting my breath as usual when I talk to you?" inquired her grandmother, flush-ing with anger.

35

"I heard what you said," said Miss Coynte, "but I have no comment to make on the story except that the little man with her would probably have suffered a broken back, if not a fracture of all bones, if Miss Dotty Reagan had fallen on top of him when he tried to catch her."

"Yes, well, the fairy had sense enough not to catch her and so his bones were not fractured."

"I see," said Miss Coynte. "Can you lie on the rubber sheet for a while till I wash some clean linen?"

"Be quick about it and bring me a bowl of strawberry sherbet and a couple of cookies," ordered the grandmother.

Miss Coynte got to the door with the soiled sheet and then she turned on her grandmother for the first time in her ten years of servitude and she said something that startled her nearly out of her wits.

"How would you like a bowl full of horseshit?" she said to the old lady, and then she slammed the door.

She had hardly slammed the door when the grandmother began to scream like a peacock in heat; she let out scream after scream, but Miss Coynte ignored them. She went downstairs and she did not wash linen for the screaming old lady. She sat on a small sofa and listened to the screams. Suddenly, one of them was interrupted by a terrific gasp.

"Dead," thought Miss Coynte.

She breathed an exhausted sigh. Then she said, "Finally."

She relaxed on the sofa and soon into her fancy came that customary flood of erotic imagination.

Creatures of fantasy in the form of young men began to approach her through the room of the first floor, cluttered with furnishings and bric-a-brac inherited from the grandmother's many dead relatives. All of these imaginary young lovers approached Miss Coynte with expressions of desire.

They exposed themselves to her as they approached, but never having seen the genitals of a male older than the year-old son of a cousin, Miss Coynte had a very diminutive concept of

36

the exposed organs. She was easily satisfied, though, having known, rather seen, nothing better.

After a few hours of these afternoon fantasies, she went back up to her grandmother. The old lady's eyes and mouth were open but she had obviously stopped breathing. . . .

Much of human behavior is, of course, automatic, at least on the surface, so there should be no surprise in Miss Coynte's actions following upon her grandmother's death.

About a week after that long-delayed event, she leased an old store on Marble Street, which was just back of Front Street on the levee, and she opened a shop there called The Better Mousetrap. She hired a black man with two mules and a wagon to remove a lot of the inherited household wares, especially the bric-a-brac, from the house, and then she advertised the opening of the shop in the daily newspaper of Greene. In the lower left-hand corner of the ad, in elegant Victorian script, she had her name, Miss Valerie Coynte, inserted, and it amazed her how little embarrassment she felt over the immodesty of putting her name in print in a public newspaper.

The opening was well attended, the name Coynte being one of historical eminence in the Delta. She served fruit punch from a large cut-glass bowl with a black man in a white jacket passing it out, and the next day the occasion was written up in several papers in that part of the Delta. Since it was approaching the Christmas season, the stuff moved well. The first stock had to be almost completely replaced after the holiday season, and still the late *Mère's* house was almost overflowing with marketable antiquities.

Miss Coynte had a big publicity break in late January, when the *Memphis Commercial Appeal* did a feature article about the success of her enterprise.

It was about a week after this favorable write-up that a young man employed as assistant manager of the Hotel Alcazar

37

crossed the street to the shop to buy a pair of antique silver salt and pepper shakers as a silver-wedding-anniversary gift for the hotel's owner, Mr. Vernon T. Silk, who was responsible for the young man's abrupt ascendancy from a job as bellhop to his present much more impressive position at the hotel.

More impressive it certainly was, this new position, but it was a good deal less lucrative, for the young man, Jack Jones, had been extraordinarily well paid for his services when he was hopping bells. He had been of a thrifty nature and after only six months, he had accumulated a savings account at the Mercantile Bank that ran into four figures, and it was rumored in Greene that he was now preparing to return to Louisiana, buy a piece of land and become a sugar-cane planter.

His name, Jack Jones, has been mentioned, and it probably struck you as a suspiciously plain sort of name and I feel that, without providing you with a full-figure portrait of him in color, executed by an illustrator of remarkable talent, you can hardly be expected to see him as clearly as did Miss Coynte when he entered The Better Mousetrap with the initially quite innocent purpose of buying those antique silver shakers for Mr. Vernon Silk's anniversary present.

Mr. Jones was a startlingly personable young man, perhaps more startlingly so in his original occupation as bellhop, not that there had been a decline in his looks since his advancement at the Alcazar but because the uniform of a bellhop had cast more emphasis upon certain of his physical assets. He had worn, as bellhop, a little white mess jacket beneath which his narrow, muscular buttocks had jutted with a prominence that had often invited little pats and pinches even from elderly drummers of usually more dignified deportment. They would deliver these little familiarities as he bent over to set down their luggage and sometimes, without knowing why, the gentlemen of the road would flush beneath their thinning thatches of faded hair, would feel an obscurely defined embarrassment that would incline them to tip Jack Jones at least double the ordinary amount of their tips to a bellhop.

Sometimes it went past that.

"Oh, thank you, suh," Jack would say, and would linger smiling before them. "Is there anything else that I can do for you, suh?"

"Why, no, son, not right now, but—"

"Later? You'd like some ice, suh?"

Well, you get the picture.

There was a certain state senator, in his early forties, who began to spend every week end at the hotel, and after midnight at the Alcazar, when usually the activities there were minimal, this junior senator would keep Jack hopping the moon out of the sky for one service after another—for ice, for booze and, finally, for services that would detain the youth in the senator's two-room suite for an hour or more.

A scandal such as this, especially when it involves a statesman of excellent family connections and one much admired by his constituency, even mentioned as a Presidential possibility in future, is not openly discussed; but, privately, among the more sophisticated, some innuendoes are passed about with a tolerant shrug.

Well, this is somewhat tangential to Miss Coynte's story, but recently the handsome young senator's wife—he was a benedict of two years' standing but was still childless—took to accompanying him on his week end visits to the Alcazar.

The lady's name was Alice and she had taken to drink.

The senator would sit up with her in the living room of the suite, freshening her drinks more frequently than she suggested, and then, a bit after midnight, seeing that Alice had slipped far down in her seat, the junior senator would say to her, as if she were still capable of hearing, "Alice, honey, I think it's beddy time for you now."

He would lift her off the settee and carry her into the bedroom, lay her gently upon the bed and slip out, locking the

39

door behind him: Then immediately he would call downstairs for Jack to bring up another bucket of ice.

Now once, on such an occasion, Jack let himself into the bedroom, not the living room door with a passkey, latched the door from inside and, after an hour of commotion, subdued but audible to adjacent patrons of the Alcazar, the senator's lady climbed out naked onto the window ledge of the bedroom.

This was just after the senator had succeeded in forcing his way into that room.

Well, the lady didn't leap or fall into the street. The senator and Jack managed to coax her back into the bedroom from the window ledge and, more or less coincidentally, the senator's week end visits to the Alcazar were not resumed after that occasion, and it was just after that occasion that Mr. Vernon Silk had promoted Jack Jones to his new position as night clerk at the hotel.

In this position, standing behind a counter in gentleman's clothes, Jack Jones was still an arrestingly personable young man, since he had large, heavy-lashed eyes that flickered between hazel and green and which, when caught by light from a certain angle, would seem to be almost golden. The skin of his face, which usually corresponds to that of the body, was flawlessly smooth and of a dusky-rose color that seemed more suggestive of an occupation in the daytime, in a region of fair weather, than that of a night clerk at the Alcazar. And this face had attracted the attention of Miss Dorothea Bernice Korngold, who had stopped him on the street one day and cried out histrionically to him: "Nijinsky, the face, the eyes, the cheekbones of the dancer Waslaw Nijinsky! Please, please pose for me as *The Specter of the Rose* or as *The Afternoon of the Faun!*"

"Pose? Just pose?"

"As the *Faun* you could be in a reclining position on cushions!"

"Oh, I see. Hmm: Uh-huh. Now, what are the rates for posing?"

"Why, it depends on the *hours!*"

"Most things do," said Jack.

"When are you *free?*" she gasped.

"Never," he replied, "but I've got afternoons off and if the rates are OK. . . ."

Well, you get the picture.

Jack Jones with his several enterprises did as well as Miss Coynte of Greene with her one. Jack Jones had a single and very clear and simple object in mind, which was to return to . southern Louisiana and to buy that piece of land, all his own, and to raise sugar cane.

Miss Coynte's purpose or purposes in life were much more clouded over by generations of dissimulation and propriety of conduct, by night and day, than those of Jack Jones.

However, their encounter in The Better Mousetrap had the volatile feeling of an appointment with a purpose; at least one, if not several purposes of importance.

She took a long, long time wrapping up the antique silver shakers and while her nervous fingers were employed at this, her tongue was engaged in animated conversation with her lovely young patron.

At first this conversation was more in the nature of an interrogation.

"Mr. Jones, you're not a native of Greene?"

"No, ma'am, I ain't. Sorry. I mean I'm not."

"I didn't think you were. Your accent is not Mississippi and you don't have a real Mississippi look about you."

"I don't have much connection with Mississippi."

"Oh, but I heard that our junior state senator, I heard it from *Mère*, was preparing you for a political career in the state."

"Senator Sharp was a very fine gentleman, ma'am, and he

did tell me one time that he thought I was cut out for politics in the state."

"And his wife, Mrs. Alice Sharp?"

"Mrs. Alice Sharp was a great lady, ma'am."

"But inclined to . . . you know?"

"I know she wanted to take a jump off the fifth-floor window ledge without wings or a parachute, ma'am."

"Oh, then *Mère* was right."

"Is this *Mère* a female hawss you are talking about who was right?"

"Yes, I think so. Tell me. How was Miss Alice persuaded not to jump?"

"Me and the senator caught ahold of her just before she could do it."

"Well, you know, Mr. Jones, I thought that this story of *Mère*'s was a piece of invention."

"If this *Mère* was a female hawss, she done a good deal of talking."

"That she did! Hmm. How long have you been in Greene?"

"I'll a been here six months and a week next Sunday coming."

"Why, you must keep a diary to be so exact about the time you arrived here!"

"No, ma'am, I just remember."

"Then you're gifted with a remarkable memory," said Miss Coynte, with a shaky little tinkle of laughter, her fingers still fussing with the wrapping of the package. "I mean to be able to recall that you came here to Greene exactly six months and a week ago next Sunday."

"Some things do stick in my mind."

"Oh!"

Pause.

"Is there a fly in the shop?"

"Fly?"

"Yes, it sounds to me like a horsefly's entered the shop!"

"I don't see no fly in the shop and I don't hear none either."

Miss Coynte was now convinced of what she had suspected.

"Then I think the humming must be in my head. This has been such a hectic week for me, if I were not still young, I would be afraid that I might suffer a stroke; you know, I really do think I am going to have to employ an assistant here soon. When I began this thing, I hadn't any suspicion that it would turn out to be such a thriving enterprise. . . ."

There was something, more than one thing, between the lines of her talk, and certainly one of those things was the proximity of this exotic young man. He was so close to her that whenever she made one of her flurried turns—they were both in front of a counter now—her fingers would encounter the close-fitting cloth of his suit.

"Mr. Jones, please excuse me for being so slow about wrapping up these things. It's just my, my—state of exhaustion, you know."

"I know."

"Perhaps you know, too, that I lost my grandmother yesterday, and—"

"Wasn't it six weeks ago?"

"Your memory *is* remarkable as. . . ."

She didn't finish that sentence but suddenly leaned back against the counter and raised a hand to her forehead, which she had expected to feel hot as fire but which was deathly cold to her touch.

"Excuse me if I. . . ."

"What?"

"Oh, Mr. Jones," she whispered with no breath in her throat that seemed capable of producing even a whisper, "if there isn't a fly, there must be a swarm of bees in this shop. Mr. Jones, you know, it was a stroke that took *Mère*."

"No, I didn't know. The paper just said she was dead."

"It was a stroke, Mr. Jones. Most of the Coyntes go that way, suddenly, from strokes due to unexpected . . . excitement. . . ."

"You mean you feel . . . ?"

"I feel like Chicken Little when the acorn hit her on the head and she said, 'Oh, the sky is falling!' I swear that's how I feel now!"

It seemed to Miss Coynte that he was about to slip an arm about her slight but sinewy waist as she swayed a little toward him, and perhaps he was about to do that, but what actually happened was this: She made a very quick, flurried motion, a sort of whirling about, so that the knuckles of her hand, lifted to just the right level, brushed over the fly of his trousers.

"Oh!" she gasped. "Excuse me!"

But there was nothing apologetic in her smile and, having completed a full turn before him, so that they were again face to face, she heard herself say to him:

"Mr. Jones, you are not completely Caucasian!"

"Not what, did you say?"

"Not completely a member of the white race?"

His eyes opened very wide, very liquid and molten, but she stood her ground before their challenging look.

"Miss Coynte, in Greene nobody has ever called me a nigger but you. You are the first and the last to accuse me of that."

"But what I said was not an accusation, Mr. Jones, it was merely—"

"Take *this*!"

She gasped and leaned back, expecting him to smash a fist in her face. But what he did was more shocking. He opened the fly that she had sensed and thrust into her hand, seizing it by the wrist, that part of him which she defined to herself as his "member." It was erect and pulsing riotously in her fingers, which he twisted about it.

"Now what does Chicken Little say to you, Miss Whitey Mighty, does she still say the sky is falling or does she say it's rising?"

"Chicken Little says the sky is rising straight up to—"

"Your tight little cunt?"

44

"Oh, Mr. Jones, I think the shop is still open, although it's past closing time. Would you mind closing it for me?"

"Leggo of my cock and I'll close it."

"Please! Do. I can't move!"

Her fingers loosened their hold upon his member and he moved away from her and her fingers remained in the same position and at the same level, loosened but still curved.

The sound of his footsteps seemed to come from some distant corridor in which a giant was striding barefooted away. She heard several sounds besides that; she heard the blind being jerked down and the catch of the latch on the door and the switching off of the two green-shaded lights. Then she heard a very loud and long silence.

"You've closed the shop, Mr. Jones?"

"That's right, the shop is closed for business."

"Oh! No!"

"By no do you mean don't?"

He had his hand under her skirt, which she had unconsciously lifted, and he was moving his light-palmed, dusky-backed, spatulate-fingered hand in a tight circular motion over her fierily throbbing mound of Venus.

"Oh, no, no, I meant do!"

It was time for someone to laugh and he did, softly.

"That's what I thought you meant. Hold still till I get this off you."

"Oh, I can't, how can I?" she cried out, meaning that her excitement was far too intense to restrain her spasmodic motions.

"Jesus," he said as he lifted her onto the counter.

"God!" she answered.

"You have got a real sweet little thing there and I bet no man has got inside it before."

"My Lord, I'm. . . ."

She meant that she was already approaching her climax.

"Hold on."

45

"Can't."

"OK, we'll shoot together."

And then the mutual flood. It was burning hot, the wetness, and it continued longer than even so practiced a stud as Jack Jones had ever known before.

Then, when it stopped, and their bodies were no longer internally engaged, they lay beside each other, breathing fast and heavily, on the counter.

After a while, he began to talk to Miss Coynte.

"I think you better keep your mouth shut about this. Because if you talk about it and my color, which has passed here so far and which has got to pass in this goddam city of Greene till I go back to buy me a piece of land and raise cane in Louisiana—"

"You are not going back to raise cane in Louisiana," said Miss Coynte with such a tone of authority that he did not contradict her, then or ever thereafter.

It was nearly morning when she recovered her senses sufficiently to observe that the front door of The Better Mousetrap was no longer locked but was now wide open, with the milky luster of street lamps coming over the sill, along with some wind-blown leaves of flaming color.

Her next observation was that she was stretched out naked on the floor.

"Hallelujah!" she shouted.

From a distance came the voice of a sleepy patrolman calling out, "Wha's that?"

Understandably, Miss Coynte chose not to reply. She scrambled to the door, locked it, got into her widely scattered clothes, some of which would barely hold decently together.

She then returned home by a circuitous route through several alleys and yards, having already surmised that her mission in life was certain, from this point onward, to involve such measures of subterfuge.

As a child in Louisiana, Jack Jones had suffered a touch of rheumatic fever, which had slightly affected a valve in his heart.

He was now twenty-five.

Old Doc Settle said to him, "Son, I don't know what you been up to lately, but you better cut down on it, you have developed a sort of noise in this right valve which is probably just functional, not organic, but we don't want to take chances on it."

A month later, Jack Jones took to his bed and never got up again. His last visitor was Miss Coynte and she was alone with him for about half an hour in Greene Memorial Hospital, and then she screamed and when his nurse went in, he was sprawled naked on the floor.

The nurse said, "Dead."

Then she glared at Miss Coynte.

"Why'd he take off his pajamas," she asked her.

Then she noticed that Miss Coynte was wriggling surreptitiously into her pink support hose, but not surreptitiously enough to escape the nurse's attention.

"I don't know what you are talking about," said Miss Coynte, although the nurse had not opened her mouth to speak a word about what Miss Coynte's state of incomplete dress implied.

It is easy to lead a double life in the Delta; in fact it is almost impossible not to.

Miss Coynte did not need to be told by any specialist in emotional problems that the only way to survive the loss of a lover such as Jack Jones had been before his collapse was to immediately seek out another; and so in the week-end edition of *The Greene Gazette*, she had inserted a small classified ad that announced very simply, "Colored male needed at The Better Mousetrap for heavy delivery service."

Bright and early on Monday morning, Sonny Bowles entered the shop in answer to this appeal.

47

"Name, please?" inquired Miss Coynte in a brisk and businesslike voice, sharply in contrast to her tone of interrogation with the late Jack Jones.

Her next question was: "Age?"

The answer was: "Young enough to handle delivery service."

She glanced up at his face, which was almost two feet above her own, to assure herself that his answer had been as pregnant with double meaning as she had hoped.

What she saw was a slow and amiable grin. She then dropped her eyes and said: "Now, Mr. Bowles, uh, Sonny, I'm sure that you understand that 'delivery service' is a rather flexible term for all the services that I may have in mind."

Although she was not at all flurried, she made one of her sudden turns directly in front of him, as she had done that late afternoon when she first met the late Jack Jones, and this time it was not her knuckles but her raised finger tips that encountered, with no pretense of accident whatsoever, the prominent something behind the vertical parabola of Sonny Bowles's straining fly.

Or should we say "Super Fly"?

He grinned at her, displaying teeth as white as paper.

Sonny turned off the green-shaded lights himself and locked the shop door himself, and then he hopped up on the counter and sat down and Miss Coynte fell to her knees before him in an attitude of prayer.

Sonny Bowles was employed at once by Miss Coynte to make deliveries in her little truck and to move stock in the store.

The closing hours of the shop became very erratic. Miss Coynte had a sign printed that said OUT TO LUNCH and that sign was sometimes hanging in the door at half past eight in the morning.

"I have little attacks of migraine," Miss Coynte explained to people, "and when they come on me, I have to put up the lunch sign right away."

Whether or not people were totally gullible in Greene,

nothing was said in her presence to indicate any suspicion concerning these migraine attacks.

The Better Mousetrap now had four branches, all prospering, for Miss Coynte had a nose for antiquities. As soon as a family died off and she heard about it, Sonny Bowles would drive her to the house in her new Roadmaster. She would pretend to be offering sincere condolences to relatives in the house, but all the while her eyes would be darting about at objects that might be desirable in her shops. And so she throve.

Sonny had a light-blue uniform with silver buttons when he drove her about.

"Why, you two are inseparable," said a spiteful spinster named Alice Bates.

This was the beginning of a feud between Miss Bates and Miss Coynte which continued for two years. Then one midnight Miss Bates's house caught fire and she burned alive in it and Miss Coynte said, "Poor Alice, I warned her to stop smoking in bed, God bless her."

One morning at ten Miss Coynte put up her OUT TO LUNCH sign and locked the door, but Sonny sat reading a religious booklet under one of the green-shaded lamps and when Miss Coynte turned the lamp off, he turned it back on.

"Sonny, you seem tired," remarked Miss Coynte.

She opened the cash register and gave him three twenty-dollar bills.

"Why don't you take a week off," she suggested, "in some quiet town like Memphis?"

When Sonny returned from there a week later, he found himself out of a job and he had been replaced in The Better Mousetrap by his two younger brothers, a pair of twins named Mike and Moon.

These twins were identical.

"Was that you, Mike," Miss Coynte would inquire after one of her sudden lunches, and then answer was just as likely to be:

"No, ma'am, this is Moon, Miss Coynte."

49

Mike or Moon would drive her in her new yellow Packard every evening that summer to the Friar's Point ferry and across it to a black community called Tiger Town, and specifically to a night resort called Red Dot. It would be dark by the time Mike or Moon would deliver Miss Coynte to this night resort and before she got out of the yellow Packard, she would cover her face with dark face powder and also her hands and every exposed surface of her fair skin.

"Do I pass inspection," she would inquire of Mike or Moon, and he would laugh his head off, and Miss Coynte would laugh along with him as he changed into his Levis and watermelon-pink silk shirt in the Packard.

Then they would enter and dance.

You know what wonderful dancers the black people are, but after a week or so, they would clear the floor to watch Miss Coynte in the arms and hands of Mike or Moon going through their fantastic gyrations on the dance floor of Red Spot.

There was a dance contest in September with a dozen couples participating, but in two minutes the other couples retired from the floor as Miss Coynte leapt repeatedly over the head of Mike or Moon, each time swinging between his legs and winding up for a moment in front of him and then going into the wildest circular motion about him that any astral satellite could dream of performing in orbit.

"Wow!"

With this exclamation Miss Coynte was accustomed to begin a dance and to conclude it also.

"Miss Coynte?"

"Yes?"

"This is Reverend Tooker."

She hung up at once and put the OUT TO LUNCH sign on the shop door, locked it up, and told Mike and Moon, "Our time is probably about to expire in Greene, at least for a while."

"At least for a while" did not mean right away. Miss Coynte was not a lady of the new South to be demoralized into precipitate flight by such a brief and interrupted phone call from a member of the Protestant clergy.

Still, she was obliged, she thought, to consider the advisability of putting some distance between herself and the small city of Greene sometime in the future, which might be nearer than farther.

One morning while she was out to lunch but not lunching, she put through a call to the chamber of commerce in Biloxi, Mississippi.

She identified herself and her name was known, even there.

"I am doing research about the racial integration of Army camps in the South and I understand that you have a large military base just outside Biloxi, and I wonder if you might be able to inform me if enlisted or drafted blacks are stationed at your camp there?"

Answer: "Yes."

"Oh, you said yes, not no. And that was the only question I had to ask you."

"Miss Coynte," drawled the voice at the other end of the phone line, "we've got this situation of integration pretty well under control, and if you'll take my word for it, I don't think that there's a need for any research on it."

"Oh, but, sir, my type of research is not at all likely to disturb your so-called control; if I make up my mind to visit Biloxi this season."

Enough of that phone conversation.

However. . . .

The season continued without any change of address for Miss Coynte. The season was late autumn and leaves were leaving the trees, but Miss Coynte remained in Greene.

51

However, changes of the sort called significant were manifesting themselves in the lady's moods and conditions.

One hour past midnight, having returned from Red Dot across the river, Miss Coynte detained her escorts, Mike and Moon, on the shadowy end of her long front veranda for an inspired conversation.

"Not a light left in the town; we've got to change that to accomplish our purpose."

"Don't you think," asked Mike or Moon, "that—"

The other twin finished the question, saying: "Dark is better for us?"

"Temporarily only," said Miss Coynte. "Now, you listen to me, Mike and Moon! You know the Lord intended something when he put the blacks and whites so close together in this great land of ours, which hasn't yet even more than begun to realize its real greatness. Now, I want you to hear me. Are you listening to me?"

"Yes, ma'am," said Mike or Moon.

"Well, draw up closer," and, to encourage them toward this closer proximity to her, she reached out her hands to their laps and seized their members like handles, so forcibly that they were obliged to draw their chairs up closer to the wicker chair of Miss Coynte.

"Someday after our time," she said in a voice as rich as a religious incantation, "there is bound to be a great new race in America, and this is naturally going to come about through the total mixing together of black and white blood, which we all know is actually red, regardless of skin color!"

All at once, Miss Coynte was visited by an apparition or vision.

Crouched upon the front lawn, arms extended toward her, she saw a crouching figure with wings.

"Lord God Jesus!" she screamed. "Look there!"

"Where, Miss Coynte?"

"Annunciation, the angel!"

Then she touched her abdomen.

"I feel it kicking already!"

The twin brothers glanced at each other with alarm.

"I wonder which of you made it, but never mind that. Since you're identical twins, it makes no difference, does it? Oh! He's floating and fading. . . ."

She rose from her chair without releasing their genitals, so that they were forced to rise with her.

Her face and gaze were uplifted.

"Goodby, goodby, I have received the Announcement!" Miss Coynte cried out to the departing angel.

Usually at this hour, approaching morning, the twins would take leave of Miss Coynte, despite her wild protestations.

But tonight she retained such a tight grip on their genital organs that they were obliged to accompany her upstairs to the great canopied bed in which *Mère* had been murdered.

There, on the surface of a cool, fresh linen sheet, Miss Coynte enjoyed a sleep of profound temporary exhaustion, falling into it without a dread of waking alone in the morning, for not once during her sleep did she release her tight hold on the handles the twins had provided—or surrendered?—win or lose being the name of all human games that we know of; sometimes both, unnamed.

Now twenty years have passed and that period of time is bound to make a difference in a lady's circumstances.

Miss Coynte had retired from business, and she was about to become a grandmother. She had an unmarried daughter, duskily handsome, named Michele Moon, whom she did not admit was her daughter but whom she loved dearly.

From birth we go so easily to death; it is really no problem unless we make it one.

53

Miss Coynte now sat on the front gallery of her home and, at intervals, her pregnant daughter would call out the screen door, "Miss Coynte, would you care for a toddy?"

"Yes, a little toddy would suit me fine," would be the reply.

Having mentioned birth and death, the easy progress between them, it would be unnatural not to explain that reference.

Miss Coynte was dying now.

It would also be unnatural to deny that she was not somewhat regretful about this fact. Only persons with suicidal tendencies are not a little regretful when their time comes to die, and it must be remembered what a full and rich and satisfactory life Miss Coynte had had. And so she is somewhat regretful about the approach of that which she could not avoid, unless she were immortal. She was inclined, now, to utter an occasional light sigh as she sipped a toddy on her front gallery.

Now one Sunday in August, feeling that her life span was all but completed, Miss Coynte asked her illegitimate pregnant and unmarried daughter to drive her to the town graveyard with a great bunch of late-blooming roses.

They were memory roses, a name conferred upon them by Miss Coynte, and they were a delicate shade of pink with a dusky center.

She hobbled slowly across the graveyard to where Jack Jones had been enjoying his deserved repose beneath a shaft of marble that was exactly the height that he had reached in his lifetime.

There and then Miss Coynte murmured that favorite saying of hers, "Chicken Little says the sky is falling."

Then she placed the memory roses against the shaft.

"You were the first," she said with a sigh. "All must be remembered, but the first a bit more definitely so than all the others."

A cooling breeze stirred the rather neglected grass.

"Time," she remarked to the sky.

And the sky appeared to respond to her remark by drawing a diaphanous fair-weather cloud across the sun for a moment with a breeze that murmured lightly through the graveyard grasses and flowers.

So many have gone before me, she reflected, meaning those lovers whom she had survived. Why, only one that I can remember hasn't gone before, yes, Sonny Bowles, who went to Memphis in the nick of time, dear child.

Miss Coynte called down the hill to the road, where she had left the pregnant unmarried daughter in curiously animated conversation with a young colored gatekeeper of the cemetery.

There was no response from the daughter, and no sound of conversation came up the hill.

Miss Coynte put on her farsighted glasses, the lenses of which were almost telescopic, and she then observed that Michele Moon, despite her condition, had engaged the young colored gatekeeper in shameless sexual play behind the family crypt of a former governor.

Miss Coynte smiled approvingly.

"It seems I am leaving my mission in good hands," she murmured.

When she had called out to her daughter, Michele Moon, it had been her intention to have this heroically profligate young lady drive her across town to the colored graveyard with another bunch of memory roses to scatter about the twin angels beneath which rested the late Mike and Moon, who had died almost as closely together in time as they had been born, one dying instantly as he boarded the ferry on the Arkansas side and the other as he disembarked on the Mississippi side with his dead twin borne in his arms halfway up the steep levee. Then she had intended to toss here and there about her, as wantonly as Flora scattered blossoms to announce the vernal season, roses in memory of that incalculable number of black lovers who had crossed the river with her from Tiger Town, but of course this intention was far more romantic than realistic, since it would have required a truckload of memory roses to serve as an adequate homage to all of those whom she had enlisted in "the mission," and actually, this late in the season, there were not that many memory roses in bloom.

Miss Coynte of Greene now leaned, or toppled, a nylon-tip pen in her hand, to add to the inscriptions on the great stone shaft one more, which would be the relevant one of the lot. This inscription was taking form in her mind when the pen slipped from her grasp and disappeared in the roses.

Mission was the first word of the intended inscription. She was sure that the rest of it would occur to her when she had found the pen among the memory roses, so she bent over to search among them as laboriously as she now drew breath, but the pen was not recovered—nor was her breath when she fell.

In her prone position among the roses, as she surrendered her breath, the clouds divided above her and, oh, my God, what she saw—

Miss Coynte of Greene almost knew what she saw in·the division of clouds above her when it stopped in her, the ability to still know or even to sense the approach of—

Knowledge of—

Well, the first man or woman to know anything finally, absolutely for sure has yet to be born in order to die on this earth. This observation is not meant to let you down but, on the contrary, to lift your spirit as the Paraclete lifted itself when—

It's time to let it go, now, with this green burning inscription: *En avant!* or "Right on!"

November 1972

Sabbatha and Solitude

Sabbatha and Solitude

"In your earlier work," wrote a former editor of the famed poetess Sabbatha Veyne Duff-Collick, "you had a certain wry touch of astringency to your flights of personal lyricism, and being such a close friend as well as your editor, whilom, I cannot help but admit to you that I am distressed to discover that that always redeeming grace of humor which, in this skeptical age, must underlie the agonies of a romanticist has somehow withheld its delicate influence on these new sonnets, admirable though they. . . ."

"Why, this old fart has gone *senile.*" Sabbatha shrieked to her audience of one, a young man whose Mediterranean aspects of character and appearance had magically survived his past ten years of sharing life with Sabbatha in her several retreats.

"Oh, he says you're senile?" the young man murmured with no evidence of surprise.

"*I* say *he* is, read *this*!—since you didn't *listen!*"

She crumpled the letter from the senior editor of Hark and Smothers and tossed it at Giovanni like a rock at a dangerous assailant, but it was only a crumpled sheet of paper and did him no injury except to distract him from certain private reflections. He was lying on his back before the open stone fireplace, his black-curled head on a throw-away pillow, he was becomingly undressed to the skin, and the fingers of a hand were scratching at the crispy bush over his genitals.

"Johnny, Johnny, Giovanni, for God's sake are you infested with lice?"

"How could I get crabs in this old birdhouse of yours unless I had 'em shipped in from—Bangor?"

Giovanni emphasized and lingered over the name of that city because those unspoken reflections which she had interrupted had to do with the city, well, not so much with the city itself but with a certain frolicsome night place in that city which was frequented mostly by men employed at gathering shellfish and who were presently barred from that employment by a phenomenon of the Maine coast that was called "the red tide," and this red tide was not a political incursion but a form of marine flora which made the shellfish inedible and therefore unmarketable when it made its appearance in the waters. This phenomenon was an economic disaster for the men who frequented the night place in Bangor but it had an appealing aspect to Giovanni, in that it would certainly increase the cordiality of his reception at the water-front bar if he should drop in there again while the "red tide" was polluting the waters: the difficulty was that the name of the place had slipped his mind and he had discovered it one night which remained quite vivid in his recollection despite a state of drunkenness that approached a mental blackout. The experiences of the night were as memorable as any in his thirty-five years and yet the name of the place and the name of the street of the place and even the general locality of the place had somehow refused to surface in his memory, which was an extremely exasperating thing to him for the night which he had spent there stood out as boldly as the Star of Bethlehem over the many, many nights of shared solitude with Sabbatha in her several retreats from the world.

Now all of a sudden the name of the night place in Bangor, Maine, flashed on the screen of his recollection with such a startling effect that he jumped up and shouted it out.

"*Sea Hag!*"

"How *dare* you!" screamed Sabbatha, thinking that he was addressing her by this name.

Of course Giovanni had addressed her by many equally un-flattering names in the course of their present long winter re-treat, and sometimes just as loudly, but she was not at this moment in a humor to tolerate any further abuse than she had suffered in the rejections of her new sonnet sequence by Hark and Smothers and a number of others.

Sabbatha retaliated to the presumed insult by kicking Giovanni's very well-turned backside with the toe of her slipper but this resulted in nothing but a stab of pain in her arthritic ankle- and knee-joints, since her slipper was a bedroom slipper of soft material and Giovanni was too comfortably insulated where she kicked him to be jolted out of his elation over re-membering the memorable night place by name.

He merely looked at Sabbatha with a sort of wolfish grin and repeated the name to fix it more sharply in his mind: "Sea Hag!"

"Son of a bitch!" she retorted, "Sea hag your ass!"

"My ass is homesick, Sabby, and this birdhouse is not the home of my ass. . . ."

He was now on his feet to get the rum bottle and slosh more rum in his tea and he drank it down chug-a-lug and then he finally turned his attention to her latest letter of rejection. He dropped back down by the fireplace and uncrumpled the letter she'd thrown at him. He read it by firelight and as he read it a mocking smile grew pleasurably over his face, which was the face of a juvenile satyr.

The firelight was dimming.

"Christ, don't you see the fire is dying out?" she demanded. "Throw more faggots in it!"

"*You* do that!"

"Cool it, lady, don't work yourself into a seizure."

He built the fire up a bit and then finished reading the letter.

"Well? No reaction? To that piece of shit?"

"There's no shit in this letter and that's what you hate about it," Giovanni told her. "All he says is you've got no humor

61

about yourself any more and he's saying also that what you're turning out now is a bunch of old repeats that no one requests any more but that you keep on repeating."

Now from his indolent attitude before the fireplace, he sprung up quick as a cat to snatch seven other letters of rejection from Sabbatha's writing table in an alcove.

Some of the letters were scarcely more than perfunctory though all were penned or dictated by "dearest," "darling" or "beloved" someone out of her professional past which had always been dangerously involved with her social past, due to the ingenuousness of her earlier nature.

"Don't" she screamed at Giovanni as if threatened by gang rape.

"Listen, shut up and listen and I'll translate these 'no-thank-you-Ma'ams' into what's back of the bullshit!"

(For a foreigner, Giovanni had picked up a startling fluency in the use of rough American idiom, mostly through his fondness for water-front bars.)

She tried to climb up his body to get the dreadful letters from his grasp but he gave her the knee and she slid off him, painfully to her.

"I will not hear them, I have never descended to . . . !"

(To what? In pursuit of what? Her moment of uncertainty and her wild glare into nothing gave him a cutting edge that he used with abandon.)

"Sabby, you'd descend to the asshole of a mole and imagine that you were rimming Apollo and you know it well as I know it!"

"What, what, what, what, what?"

(With each "what" she had crawled a pace toward the door, she was now scrambling toward it, almost.)

But all of her motions, now, were subject to arthritis, so she was still short of the door when she collapsed and rolled onto her back and cried out: *"Time!"*

"Yeh, yeh, time has fucked you, with its fickle finger, let's face it, Sabby!"

She managed to get the door open.

"I shall go out and stay out till you've drunk yourself into oblivion as usual, and then I shall make the—necessary arrangements. . . ."

What these arrangements might be was a speculation lost in her dizzy flight from the cottage called "Sabbatha's Eyrie."

Sabbatha's Eyrie was one and a half stories of weathered shingles, all mottled white and gray as a sea gull's wings or as her own chestnut hair became when she neglected the beauty shop for a full season as she had done during these past few months of relentless work upon her new sonnet sequence. It stood, the Eyrie, upon the height of the highest and craggiest promontory on that section of New England seacoast. Among its appropriately lyrical assets was a pure narrow brook and it was to this brook that she now took flight, unconsciously hoping that its subdued murmurs of excitement would evoke voices from the past, the sort of excited whispers that she used to hear, for instance, when she would enter a certain little French restaurant in the Village, when Sabbatha was a pre-eminent figure in the literary world and the world of fashion as well.

Oh, yes, the pine wood through which she fled toward the brook was already full of voices, all in reference to her.

"Christ, I must be a little drunk," she admitted to herself as she staggered among those trees which she thought of some-times as her "sylvan grove," and she was literally toppling from the support of one tree to that of another, and, oh, less than ten years ago, just after the importation of Giovanni from Italy, she had used to run like a nymph in her flowing white night-dress through these woods, crying back to him, "Catch me if you can!"

And of course he could but he didn't, in fact she would often find that he had returned to be when she returned, winded, to Sabbatha's Eyrie. "Sleep, darling," she would whisper a little crossly and certainly not sincerely, for she would make sure that her wanton caresses interrupted his sleep. She particularly liked to gather his testicles in her hand and to squeeze them spasmodically.

"*Senta!*" he'd shout. "You are not milking a cow!"

"The moon is bone white at daybreak," she would whisper with her tongue in his ear, and often, after some such remark as that, she would scramble from bed to compose a sonnet beginning with such a line.

In a lecture at Vassar, or rather at the conclusion of her lecture when the students were invited to ask her questions, one young lady there had inquired impertinently if she didn't feel that there was too much erotic material in her sonnets.

"Whatever's included in life," she had shot back at the girl, "must be included in art, and if there is eroticism in my work, it is because my existence does not reject it!"

Her head was full of memory tonight, and effect of red wine.

"I must chill my veins in the spring," she advised herself. "I must go back to Giovanni chill and damp from the spring and have him dry me off with one of the big rough towels, and all things will be as they were. . . ."

How were they, that was the question, but it was not a question to be entertained at this moment. Her erratic course through the pine woods had now brought her to the spring.

"I can still walk barefooted through cold water, over rough stones," she assured herself. Then she flung off her felt bedroom slippers and stepped into the rapid, murmurous current of the brook.

Tonight it was practically babbling those voices out of the past.

She heard excitedly amplified whispers such as she used to hear in her favorite little French restaurant in the Village before she'd imported Giovanni (and Sabbatha's Eyrie to keep him in), yes, quite a while before then, at least twenty years.

In those days she had always been escorted by a bevy of very young men, and she had marched into the restaurant, oh, yes, it was called *L'Escargot Fou,* ahead of her feverishly animated escorts, and at once, in those early days, a few moments of hush would descend upon "the mad snail," as she called it.

Then, as she was seated at her corner table, voices would become audible, exclaiming about her.

"That striking woman, who is she?"

"Christ, don't you know her? Sabbatha Veyne Duff-Collick?"

"I *thought* so, but wasn't quite sure! Are these young men all her *lovers?*"

"Yes, of course, she's the most profligate artist since Isadora Duncan."

"She does move like a dancer, she has a dancer's gestures, and what a distinguished profile with that long mane of chestnut hair."

And then they would talk about other matters which concerned themselves, but seated among her bevy of youths in a corner, she knew that they were all really talking so loudly in order that she could hear them, and she would smile indulgently to herself at their innocent folly.

But, oh, my God, there was that final visit to "the mad snail" when she had entered to find her usual table usurped by some very scrubby and bearded young men, not at all the sort that she went about with.

"Maître," she had said, "my table is occupied by strangers tonight. Would you please remove them for me?"

"Oh, madam," the maître replied, "that is the young poet Ginsberg with two others, they can't be moved, I'm afraid they'd make a scene if I asked them to give up the table. You see, they're very, very fashionable just now. They've been on the covers of several big magazines lately."

"Why, one of those obscene barbarians is seated in the very chair that has the bronze plate with my *name* engraved on it! Always reserved for *meeeee!*"

"Plate? Bronze? Engraved?" the maître repeated in a mock tone of incredulity. Then his face assumed a look of recollection and he said, "Oh, you must mean the chair that collapsed and couldn't be repaired, it did have an old piece of metal on the back, but it's gone to the junkyard now."

"You must be new here to speak to me in this insolent way."

"I've not been around as long as some of our patrons, but as they say about brooms, a new one sweeps clean, madam."

At this she had drawn herself up and thrown her head back so far that she seemed to be inspecting the ceiling.

"I wouldn't speak of cleanliness, I would avoid that subject in view of your new clientele! Come along, *mes amis!* When an eating place turns into a trough for swine, I. . . ."

She didn't complete this statement for the group of poets who had confiscated her table burst into howls of derision: her young men shepherded her quickly onto the street.

"*Cochons!*" she screamed.

The streets of the Village spun brilliantly about her for a moment before everything went black. When she came to, she had only one young man with her: they were in a taxi, headed uptown. He was a very slight young man with great sorrowful eyes, and he carried a small beaded bag.

"Oh, Sabbatha," he whispered, "didn't God tell you that things turn out this way?"

"I have received no information from God except that I am alive and capable of decision. Tomorrow I am going to Paris and then to Venice and then to The Eternal City of Rome."

"Will you take me with you?"

She sighed and permitted her hand to fall into his lap. And there she made a discovery of less than minimal requirements for a long-term companion.

"My dear," she murmured, "how dreadful it must be for you."

He understood her meaning and after a moment or two he said to her: "I have some male friends of your age or thereabouts who have admired the size and color of my eyes."

66

"God help you, dear, in this world. God help your large eyes, these friends will gouge them out."

And they both began to cry quietly together with clasped hands.

At the dockside in Cherbourg, many cameras were focused on Sabbatha as she disembarked and the effect was exhilarating to her.

Apparently Europe was not yet aware of her declining prestige or it had more respect for work not favored by trivial fashion.

A journalist in Rome. . . .

"How does it feel to be the most celebrated female poet since Sappho?"

"Of Sappho's work," she replied, looking into space, "there remain only fragments, such as. . . ."

At the moment she couldn't think of any.

"Miss Duff-Collick, your work is sometimes compared to. . . ."

"Oh, yes, I know whom you mean and, actually, I did rather like the one about some birds and beasts. How did it go? Something about entertaining no charitable hope. And it rhymed with *antelope*! . . . I've always liked wild animals in their natural habitats, not domestic ones or the pathetic creatures in zoos. I detest confinement, you know. . . ."

"Your work in the sonnet form has naturally suggested to some critics the influence of Elizabeth Barrett Browning."

"My dear young man," she laughed. "My influence on Mrs. Browning must have been rather slight since she succumbed to consumption long before I was born."

This interview was taking place in a little *taverna* where the Via Margutta angles sharply into the Piazza de Spagna. There were three young journalists and there was also the young painter Giovanni. He had been in the *taverna* when she and the newspaper people entered and she had greeted him as if she knew him well the moment that she first saw him and had invited him to join the group at her table.

She sensed that her behavior was leading her into public embarrassment. She even suspected that she might be going a little crazy but the thought gave her no alarm: in fact, it exhilarated her as the flash bulbs had when she arrived in Europe.

She had arranged the seating at the table and placed Giovanni next to her.

"You've found some one you know?"

"Oh, yes, I'm sure we've known each other forever."

She decided to expand upon that typically histrionic remark.

"All of my first encounters with people are like that, as if I'd known and hated them forever or as if I'd known and loved them since before I was born."

The journalists exchanged inscrutable glances but she paid no heed.

She had a hand on Giovanni's arm and then on his knee and she made certain that the newspaper people observed this exhibition of poetic license or whatever it might be termed.

They all drank golden Frascati out of big carafes.

Going mad can have a certain elation to it if you don't fight it, if you just pull out all the stops, heedless of consequence.

Sabbatha knew this was happening to her and offered no resistance, with flash cameras popping in her face while pencils scribbled comments for press release, here in a Roman *taverna* so close to the house in which John Keats had written of love and death in lines which almost approached the intensity of her own.

For ten years she had been much out of the public eye and, phonetically, there is slight difference between the noun "decade" and the adjective "decayed," just an accent placed on the first syllable or the second.

Then came a devastatingly brutal question from the young journalist with the most innocent and deferential air.

"Does it disturb you much, Miss Duff-Collick, that your most celebrated poem was written while you were still at the female college of Bryn Mawr?"

The heavy carafe felt very light in her hand as she lifted it from the table and shattered it over the head of the young man who had stabbed her with that insufferable question.

By midnight she had proposed to Giovanni that he remain with her permanently.

He told her that he was a poor young student of painting whose survival depended upon the interest of an elderly patron. But, as Sabbatha guessed, this plaint was only a token of reluctance. . . .

(In those days all the young and impoverished Romans dreamt of being spirited off to the States.)

At daybreak they engaged a horse-drawn vehicle, a fiacre with a hunchback driver.

She touched the driver's hump for luck which made him furious. He turned about and shouted in her face, *"Che vecchia strega, che stronza!"*

"What did he say? Something impertinent to me?"

"He called you a witch," said Giovanni, discreet enough that first night between them, not to translate the scatalogical portion of the old man's invective.

"I'll show him when we get to San Pietro!"

At Saint Peter's Square she had Giovanni direct the hunchback to drive about the twin fountains and when he hesitated to comply Sabbatha scrambled over the partition between passengers and driver and wrenched the reins from the driver's hands.

He leapt out of the carriage and started shouting, *"Polizia!"*

Sabbatha stood up like a Roman charioteer, tore her blouse open to expose her rather flat and pendulous breasts and drove the horses round and round the fountains till she was drenched in the windy spray and was almost restored to sobriety.

But this incident proved to be one touch of poetic license too much for public tolerance in The Eternal City.

The next morning it was reported scathingly in *Il Messagero* that a demented female tourist, with a much younger male companion of questionable morals, had made a *"bruta figura"* in the sacred square and that she would be well advised to indulge her inebriate fancies in some other province if not in a madhouse.

Once again, then, and for the last time in her European sojourn, she was confronted by cameras and reporters. It was when she came out of the lift at the Academy.

"About the scandal?" they asked her.

"All truth is a scandal," she informed them in ringing tones, "and all art is an indiscretion!"

With this outcry she had tossed her hair in their faces and lifted her arms in a gesture which she thought the cameras would interpret as an unfettered condition of spirit as strikingly as the camera of Genthe had captured for posterity the classic pose of Isadora Duncan among the columns of the Acropolis: but evidently there was a difference both in the subject and in the photographic craft or intention, for what appeared next day in the papers of Rome suggested nothing more nor less than the abandoned posturing of a middle-aged female, three or four sheets to the wind.

A day later she left Rome with Giovanni who recognized her manic condition quite clearly, now, but was adhered to the lady as a postage stamp to an incoherent post card.

In the early days of film-making the copulation of lovers could only be suggested by some such device as cutting from a preliminary embrace to a bee hovering over the chalice of a lily: and there is probably a similar bit of artifice involved in bringing up so much of Sabbatha's past history through the murmurs of the spring that cascaded beneath her Eyrie.

In any case, those evocative murmurs of the spring were now invaded and quite overwhelmed by another sound, the starting of a motor which was that of Giovanni's sports car, the Triumph she'd given him on his thirty-fifth birthday that summer. It was roaring into motion.

At its first noise she had cried out, "Giovanni!" and had made a staggering rush to intercept the car in the drive winding down from her Eyrie, but of course wasn't quick enough to throw herself across the drive before the car had passed over the wooden bridge and was beyond interception: indeed, she wondered if, had she been able to throw herself in the car's way, he might not have driven it straight over her prostrate body, and gone on speeding away.

The sound of the motor receded and receded, now, until it faded under the *tristesse* of the brook, and Sabbatha and solitude had at last joined forces truly, if forces is the right word for it.

The first night that Sabbatha found herself unable to ascend the stairs to the bedroom in a reasonably vertical state, in other words as a biped, but had to mount them on all fours if she wished to sleep in bed, she assumed with some logic that she was entering upon a downstairs existence at Sabbatha's Eyrie. She realized that her curvature of the spine which now made it difficult to reach objects on a mantel or kitchen shelf without the precarious expedient of climbing onto a tabletop or a chair, articles of furniture that seemed to resent her efforts to climb on them as female animals not in heat resent the advances of the tumescent males of their species, it occurred to her that death in solitude was not an unlikely or remote prospect, and this reflection was entertained by the lady with mixed emotions.

Death in solitude, she remarked to herself, rolling her sea-green eyes from side to side in their sockets, set rather close together on either side of her almost too prominent nose.

Names of poets and poetesses who had died alone, completely alone or virtually alone, passed through her mind. It was a roll call of honor: it included such names as Thomas Chatterton who had hung himself alone in his garret to escape debtor's prison, it included the minor but not ungifted poetess Sara Teasdale who had cut her wrists in a bathtub, presumably behind a locked door without bath attendants, it included that eccentric spinster poetess, somewhere between minor and major, who had died alone in agony from a deliberate O.D. of some nonlycergic acid, and now it seemed to Sabbatha that death in solitude was the preordained fate of almost any self-respecting poet or poetess.

On hands and knees she had reached the telephone stand on the stair landing when this sad but uplifting conviction took hold of her.

She was just barely able to haul the phone off its stand and from a prostrate condition she put through a long-distance call to one of her once-young male escorts in Manhattan. He was still living there and was now employed as a society reporter for the leading newspaper. The call was put through with difficulty and through his answering service. It took her almost an hour and a great deal of shrieking and growling to track him down at the residence of the Fourth Duchess of Argyle, and when she finally had him on the wire, she could scarcely make her voice, strong as it remained, heard through the hysteria of supper guests of the Duchess, all high on grass or booze with Rock music. The former young escort kept pretending to think, or did actually think, that he was receiving a crank call: she only succeeded in confirming her identity to him by reciting the sextet of a sonnet which he had once pronounced her most exquisite accomplishment of all.

"Oh, yes, then it *is* you, Sabbatha. How *goes* it?"

"My darling, I am preparing myself for death in complete solitude which is why I am calling to beg you to . . . *wait! I'm all choked up!* Preston, I know that important newspapers keep a file of obituaries of well-known persons, especially when the person's health is known to be failing. Now, Preston, this is dreadfully vain of me but I can't help but want to know what is going to be printed about me when I. . . . Do you understand, darling? And could you very, very privately obtain a copy of my obituary from these secret files called obits? Please, please I can't explain how or why it would matter so much to me, but somehow it does, it really and truly does, so for old time's sake, would you, could you, please, do this for me, dearest?"

"Sabbatha, you are breaking my heart," he said rather matter-of-factly. "Why just last month I saw a little squib for your new book of verse, *The Bride's Bouquet*, cute title. And now you want me to sneak your obit out of the files? My God, you've broken my rice bowl! I have to blow my mind with another joint, baby. Take care, *ciao, bambina!*"

He had hung up with a bang, but a few days later a letter arrived whose envelope bore the masthead of his newspaper.

Thus far this top-secret letter had remained unopened at the Eyrie but she knew precisely where it was, she'd put it under a box of Twining's Formosa Oolong tea bags in the breakfast nook.

It took considerable time and effort for her to retrieve it since the chair fell over several times before she could success-fully mount it.

It also took her quite a while to get the obit into the living (or dying) room where she had intended to read it by firelight

73

which she had somehow imagined might improve her reaction
to its content.

But nothing could have assuaged her shock when she saw
that the clipping was less than half a column in length and
included no photograph of her and that it had even dared to
omit one 'b' from Sabbatha and the hyphen between Duff and
Collick.

Fuck them all! she decided. *Fuck them all, past, present and
future!*

She flung the obit into the appropriately dying embers where
it revived a slight and brief conflagration before going up in
smoke—as human vanity must either side of—

The nocturnal *fiasco* of California *Chianti* served Sabbatha
now as a measure of the hours before detested daylight crept
between the locked shutters of her Eyrie. When the bottle was
half empty it would be about midnight and when there were
only two or three inches left in it, she knew that she might at
any instant expect the crow of a distant cock to warn her that
it was time to chug-a-lug the remaining vino and bury her face
in the nest of cushions she'd hauled down from the sofa several
months ago to provide her with pillow and mattress.

Beside this disordered bed before the fireplace were the implements of her trade, the notebooks and pencils, now that
the arthritic condition of her joints had obliged her to give up
the Underwood portable whose ribbon, anyway, had faded to a
point where a typed page had become barely legible.

It is hardly fair to speak of notebooks and pencils as the implements of her trade, and yet that's how she thought of them:
she had come to think of the composition of Elizabethan and
Petrarchan sonnets as a trade in the sense that the trade of
Jesus of Nazareth had been carpentry. Notebooks and pencils,
hammers and nails: in the end, crucifixion, an honorable though
God-awful painful way to get out of mortal existence.

74

Going out alone, prostrate before a dead fire, Father, why hast Thou?

The distant cock had crowed and she had stretched out a hand curved as a hook toward the nearly empty *fiasco* and had upset it so that the remnant of wine was spilt upon a cushion.

Quickly, with a famished "hah," she pressed her mouth to the purple pool and lapped it up with her tongue. "Hah," she said once more, and was about to bury her head in the moist pillow when into her mind flashed the final quatrain of what must have been an early lyric of hers since she couldn't remember its title nor the preceding lines of it.

She clutched at a pencil and made a trembling tight fist of her hand about that implement to scrawl into the nearest notebook this bit of verse that bore so clearly the stamp of her springtime vigor of expression.

> *In masks outrageous and austere*
> *The years go by in single file*
> *Yet none has merited my fear*
> *And none has quite escaped my smile.*

She waited and waited till the blue of daybreak slit through the shutters for the rest to come back to her: it would, and indeed it did, and the fact that she remembered the fact that it was a fragment of a poem by Miss Elinor Wylie was a fact that completely escaped her smile and almost merited her afternoon-long depression.

Curvature of the spine!

The physical being pointing itself remorsely back toward earth.

More and more bending itself back that way, as if the earth had flung a welcoming door wide open for its timorous guest.

Clearly things had not followed an ascending line at Sabbatha's Eyrie during her time of all but total seclusion. She had not heard from Giovanni, not at all directly, but last week a bank official in Bangor had informed her by mail that a young man of a foreign extraction had been forging checks on her name there. He claimed, said this official, to be her husband but admitted that they were now permanently separated: and there had been other complaints about him of a nature that the bank official preferred not to discuss with a lady. He did tell Sabbatha that the young man had been jailed several times and hospitalized also. Of course the bank was interested only in the matter of the forged checks. Did she wish to have him prosecuted? They understood that he was not actually her husband but a former employee, and, given her approval of such action, they could have him put away for at least a year, maybe more.

She got through to the bank by telephone and told them that the young man was not a former employee but her husband by common law.

How large were the checks, she inquired, and for what had the gifted but unbalanced young man been hospitalized, was it a serious condition or—

"Madam," said the official, "I doubt that a lady would care for specific information of this nature."

"All truth," Sabbatha told him, "is scandal. Why not?"

He may or may not have understood this epigrammatic comment on "truth" but it was obvious to him that her voice was deep in drink. . . .

How to go on? You go on, in solitude, implements of the trade turned treacherous to you or you to them, cocks crowing thrice before daybreak, detestable as a jail-keeper to the condemned, the whole bit, on you go with it, don't you?

"Oh, my Lord, I don't believe I ordered my instant freeze-dried from Hollow Market and I've run completely out. Oh, my Lord, oh, *shit*. . . ."

She said this aloud, not having heard the approach of a taxi from the village, the shutting of its door and the opening of the front door of the Eyrie behind her aching back.

"Sabbatha, that's the first time I ever heard you say shit."

It was the voice of Giovanni, or was she out of her senses?

She rolled over with a crunching sound in her pelvis and there above her stood—no, not Giovanni but the ghost of him, it seemed! He looked ethereal, but not poetically so, and his youthful appearance was gone.

"Oh, my Lord, is that really *you*, Giovanni?"

"Is that really *you*, Sabbatha?"

Very slowly, it must have taken a full minute, they came to accept the present realities of each other's condition without further speech between them.

When she spoke again she said to him: "I understand you have been ill and hospitalized since you left me?"

"Yes, fucked too much," he answered. "It's possible, you know, to get too much of a good thing sometimes."

Again the conversation between them stopped for close to a minute.

"I didn't understand what you said about your illness."

"I developed a fistula," he said.

"A what did you say you developed?"

He threw off his coat and crouched in front of her and repeated the word to her loudly, separating the syllables.

"I've never heard of that. Fist full of what did you say?

He grinned at her then.

"I didn't say fist full of nothing, I said a fistula which is a perforation of the mucous membrane that lines the rectum and I got it from being gang-banged in Bangor, ten cocks up my

77

ass in one night and one of them a yard long. Now did you hear me, did you understand me that time?"

"I don't know medical terms, you know, dear," said Sabbatha. "I'm afraid I've finished the wine but there's some rum in the kitchen and some tea bags and why don't you take off those wet things and dry off in front of the fire."

"The fire's out," he told her.

"Oh, well, if it's burned out there's dry logs and pine cones under the shed. You fix your drink and undress and I'll crawl out for the wood."

She did start to crawl but he stopped her.

"Jesus, woman, have you turned into a snake?"

"Giovanni, I am the Serpent of the Nile," she replied. "And you are Anthony but our fleet has been defeated and scuttled in the harbor of Alexandria."

Apparently some of her old wry humor had returned.

She twisted her neck, which made a creaking noise, and cried out, "Charmine, fetch me the ass!"

After a moment she smiled sleepily and corrected herself: "I meant the asp, of course, dear."

June 1973

Completed

Completed

Although Miss Rosemary McCool was approaching the age of twenty she had yet to experience her first menstruation. This was surely a circumstance that might have given pause to her widowed mother's intention that season of presenting her daughter, an only child, to the society of Vicksburg, Mississippi, since presenting a girl to society amounts to publicly announcing that she is now eligible for union in marriage and the bearing of offspring.

This being the situation you might suspect the widow McCool of harboring a marked degree of duplicity or delusion in her nature, but such a suspicion, like many suspicions about genteel Southern matrons, would not be fair to the widow, for Rosemary's mother was so caught up in her multitude of social and civic and cultural activities throughout the southern Delta, all of which seemed important to her as the world itself and human life in the world, that it simply seemed to the widow that it was socially meet and proper for her daughter to make a debut and what, then, should deter it.

Of course, "Miss Sally" McCool could not be described as a very devoted and conscientious mother. In fact every time her eyes rested briefly on her daughter, she had to repress a look of trouble and disappointment, if not of personal aggrievement. Even for Miss Sally McCool it was impossible not to admit that Rosemary was an odd-looking girl, very pale and gangling and certainly not endowed with an aura of being much involved with a world of externals. She had the face, especially the eyes, of a frightened little girl, and her Aunt Ella, the widow's older sister, was the only person to whom Rosemary could speak in a voice much above a whisper. This vocal inhibition had naturally been a detriment to her in the Vicksburg high school, such a considerable detriment, in fact, that during her last year there the superintendent had called on the widow McCool and after a lot of effusive guff about her daughter's sweet and charming nature, had announced that Rosemary was simply not suited for the sort of schooling that the high school could give her and that it was his opinion that she should be transferred to a small private school which was called Mary, Help a Christian.

Miss Sally had stared at him open mouthed for a minute without producing a sound except a slight gasp.

He had returned the stare without flinching and had interrupted the silence with a sympathetic remark.

"I know that this suggestion must come to you as a bit of a shock, Miss Sally, but I can assure you personally that this precious young girl of yours is just not adjusting at all to her teachers and schoolmates at Vicksburg High. I'm sorry, Miss Sally, but nobody at the high school knows what to make of the child and I would be very dishonest if I didn't report this to you, privately, here in your house, and suggest Mary, Help a Christian as the best if not only solution I can think of."

The discussion continued a good deal further than that but it resulted exactly as the Vicksburg High superintendent had intended it should and Rosemary was transferred almost at once to Mary, Help a Christian. However, even there, with teachers trained and accustomed to dealing with problem students, Rosemary had shown no improvement in adjustment. While many of the students were irrepressibly outspoken, Rosemary still could not be asked a question by a teacher but had to be graded entirely upon her written work. Of course some of the teachers ignored this vocal inhibition and would sometimes ask her a question. On these awful occasions Rosemary would crouch low in her seat, breathe noisily and raise a trembling hand to her lips as if to indicate that she was a mute. Her written work was not much help in the matter. Her essays were childishly written, her spelling was atrocious, and her handwriting barely legible due to a nervous tremor of her fingers. A condition like this ought to have met with some sympathy but there was something about Rosemary that drew no sympathy toward her, neither among her elders, nor those of her own generation or younger. Not only did she fail to make any friends, she barely made any acquaintances. She seemed determined and destined to slip through the world as an all but unseen and unheard being.

This is harking back half a year, but it is too pertinent to her history to be excluded. Once in her English class at Mary, Help a Christian, she submitted a long, laborious and illegible essay on the assigned subject "My Purpose in Life." This essay was rejected by the English teacher, it was returned to Rosemary with a note that demanded she condense it to a few sentences, write it in print, and adhere precisely to the assigned subject. Miss Rosemary did exactly that. In very large printed letters she wrote not just a few sentences but one sentence only, which sentence was shakily printed out as follows: "I HAVE NO PURPOSE IN LIFE EXCEP COMPLETE IT QUIK AS POSIBLE FOR ALL CONSERNED IF ANY BESIDE MY ANT ELLA."

Reading this one-sentence essay on Rosemary's purpose in life, the English teacher marked it A plus and added the marginal question: "Who is your 'Ant' Ella?"

Now about Rosemary's sexual malfunction, her failure to menstruate as she neared twenty and her presentation to society in the Grand Hotel ballroom of Vicksburg, this was a considerable peculiarity but it remained a thing that neither Miss Sally nor her daughter had ever discussed. Miss Sally`was a Southern lady of the sort that considered such matters outside the pale of discussion, even between a mother and a daughter who was her only child, and so she sailed right ahead with her plans for the girl's presentation to society.

The occasion came off, in the sense that it occurred, but it was not only a pathetic affair but a distinctly bizarre one. It was attended mostly by Miss Sally's middle-aged club-women associates and they attended it as if it were a spectator sport.

Whispering on the sidelines, they said such things as this:

"Imagine bringing out a girl like that one!"

"I have never known a girl more suited for staying in!"

Of course, there was a cluster of younger folks in the ballroom but most of them suggested rare species of birds.

The local society editor was there and her comment wasn't whispered.

"I don't know how on earth I am going to write this thing up."

This "thing" in the hotel ballroom didn't last very long: it was cut short by an encounter between Rosemary and a skinny young man of whom it was rumored that he suffered from a physiological deficiency that was somewhat analogous to hers. He was called Pip or Pippin, as a nickname, and his rumored deficiency was that his testes had never descended and that this was the reason he spoke in such a high, thin voice and had never shaved in his twenty-two years.

But Pippin was a young man as animated as Rosemary was reserved, and when the colored band struck up their opening number, which was "Beale Street Blues," he rushed over to Rosemary as if shot out of a cannon, shrieking "May I have the pleasure?" and before she had a chance to deny him the pleasure, he clutched her about the waist and attempted violently to move the girl onto the dance floor.

"*Let! Me! Go!*" she screamed.

It was a preposterous incident to occur at a debut party, and the party began to break up at once.

Rosemary was silently furious with her mother for having

inflicted this embarrassment on her and had gone to her Aunt Ella's house with no intention of returning home ever.

Aunt Ella had always provided Rosemary with a retreat in times of crisis. She was Miss Sally's much older sister and she called Rosemary "dear child." She occupied a little frame house on the outskirts of town, and was attended by a Negro woman whose voice was soft as a dove's. At Aunt Ella's everything was soft, the lights, the beds, the voices: Aunt Ella had no doorbell and no telephone, she'd had them removed long ago from her weathered blue-shuttered frame residence as abscessed teeth are removed to avoid a poisoning of the system. She also received no publications of any kind, not even the town newspaper, her excuse being that she didn't wish to be informed of changes in the world since she suspected that there was nothing good in them. The shutters were kept almost completely closed day and night and although the house had once been wired for electric current, Miss Ella had permitted all the light bulbs except the one in the kitchen to burn out and had never replaced them since she preferred the light of oil lamps and candles. Receiving no news of births, marriages or deaths, she would refer to middle-aged matrons and grandmothers by their maiden names and she would speak of the dead as if they were still living, which she usually supposed them to be. Her connection with the world was elderly black Susie who did all her marketing for her, and if Susie received any reports of goings on abroad, she was wise enough to maintain a silence about them in Aunt Ella's presence.

"Child, Rosemary, whenever you're tired of that idiotic social business at Sister's, just pack a bag and move out here with old Susie and me. The whole upstairs is vacant. I can't climb steps any more but Susie can get it ready whenever you want it and there's also your Grandfather Cornelius Dunphy's comfortable little room which he occupied down here when he couldn't climb steps any more and, you know, Rosemary, dear child, it's been fifty years since I've received a post card from him at that

85

veteran's hospital in Jackson so I have a suspicion that since he was over sixty when he went there, he may be resting now with Grandmother on Cedar Hill. Your mother may know about that if she knows about anything but pieces of local gossip not fit for a lady to know. . . ."

Rosemary had heard variations of this soft monotone, so much like the sound a moth makes against a screen at dusk, so repeatedly that she could whisper it to herself like a memorized psalm, and there were times when it was seductive to her. . . .

There is much to be said for the exclusion of violent sound from the world. Aunt Ella's house was not far from the airport but Aunt Ella did not seem to know about the airport and when she heard a plane fly over she would call out softly, "Susie, fasten the shutters tight, there's going to be a thunder shower, I reckon."

"Yais, Miss Ella, I'll do that, don't you worry."

(But of course she didn't and Miss Ella may well have known that she didn't, since once, in Rosemary's presence, she had given a little wink right after this warning about the approach of a thunder shower.)

Once a week, Sunday nights, Rosemary had supper at Aunt Ella's. There was not much variation in these Sunday evening suppers, there would always be boiled chicken with dumplings, cooked till the chicken meat was falling off the bones in deference to Aunt Ella's chronic gastritis and badly fitted dentures, a bowl full of turnip greens seasoned with salt pork, sticks of lightly toasted corn pone, and either blancmange for dessert or floating island, all of it soft and monotonous as Aunt Ella's talk. The table linen and silver were of lovely quality and Aunt Ella's talk was nearly always about the goodness of The Holy Mother and discrepancies which she had noted in the Scriptures according to the Apostles.

One Sunday evening supper Rosemary had brought up a concern of her own. It had to do with a comic valentine she had received which addressed her as "Miss Priss."

"Oh, dear child," Aunt Ella had interrupted, raising a hand as if to dismiss an intruder, "some people do such things, why, once your Grandfather Cornelius Dunphy, drinking wine at supper, raised his glass to me and said, 'Here's to your ever-lasting virginity, old Miss, if you know what I mean,' and, well, I knew what he meant, you'd be surprised how much I have managed to know in the way of unwelcome as well as welcome knowledge in the course of my seventy-five or six years on this evil planet, so I simply bowed to him slightly and raised my glass of ice water and said, 'Why, thank you, Sir, I have every reason to hope that my maiden state will continue to defy whatever conspiracy may be offered against it,' and I must say that gave him quite a good, long laugh. Oh, dear, it was just a week later that he left the house for that Veterans' Place in Jackson from which he never returned and has sent me no written message. Oh, I do trust that he has mended his ways, that is, if he isn't now resting on Cedar Hill with your saintly Grandmother, and now, dear child, if you will push my wheel chair into the parlor, we'll allow Susie to clear the supper dishes and tidy up the kitchen."

Sometimes out of these soft monotones at Aunt Ella's there would emerge a note of philosophy that was far from super-ficial.

"Now, dear child," she'd once said, "the more that the world outside is excluded, the more the interior world has space in which to increase. Some spinsters enter convents to find this out, but I regard my house as a place of devotion to all that I hold dear, and every evening, soon as I see blackness through the shutters and take my little tablet of morphine, I have Susie set a rocking chair by the bedside and I want you to know that Our Lady has never failed to enter the bedroom almost imme-diately after Susie goes out. She comes in and She sits down in Her rocker as if it were Her throne in Heaven, and She turns to me and smiles at me so sweetly, lifting her right hand in benediction, that I close my eyes on tears of indescribable peace and happiness, no matter what pains afflict me, and then I drift into sleep. She never leaves till I do. . . ."

Soon after Rosemary's reluctant return to her mother's house, she experienced her first menstrual period. When she suddenly found her bed sheets stained with this initial sign of fertility, she had run sobbing out of the house, all the way to Aunt Ella's on foot, through alleys mostly, until she had reached the outskirts of town, and she had arrived before Aunt Ella had slept off her morphine. She had run into Aunt Ella's bed-room and collapsed into the chair reserved for Our Lady's noc-turnal visits and had cried out to Aunt Ella, "Oh, Aunt Ella, I'm bleeding!"

"Child, get out of Our Lady's chair," was Aunt Ella's drugged response to this outcry.

Black Susie was now looming in the doorway.

"Miss Ella, the child says she's bleeding."

Miss Ella rose up slowly on her mound of pillows as if reluctantly emerging from a protective state.

"Is she out of Our Lady's chair, Susie?"

"Yes, Ma'am, she's out of the chair and leaning against the wall and shaking all over."

"Well, now, what's wrong with her now?"

"Aunt Ella, I'm bleeding to death!"

"What did she say, Susie? Her voice is so different I can't tell what she's saying."

"She says she's bleeding to death."

"I don't see any cut on her."

"It's not on my face, it's—!"

"Where are you bleeding from, child?"

Rosemary felt as she had felt in a classroom at Mary, Help a Christian when she was asked a question that demanded a spoken answer and she couldn't give one, and so she resorted to gestures, she covered her eyes with one hand, then slowly and tremulously lowered the other hand to her groin.

Miss Ella was now rising out of her opiate cloud.

"Oh, there, she means there. Is this for the first time, child?"
Rosemary nodded her head several desperate times.

"What did she say, Susie?"

"She nodded her head, Miss Ella. I reckon she means she never had it before."

"How old are you, child?" asked Aunt Ella.

Susie answered for her: "She's about twenty, Miss Ella."

"Yes, well, peculiar. Isn't it like my fool sister never to have warned her of the curse which usually afflicts a female person five or six years before twenty."

"We know Miss Sally," said Susie, in her dove-soft voice.

"Yes, we know her too well. I think she gave this child a debut party on the roof of a hotel, which upset her like this, I think you told me so, Susie."

"No, Miss Ella, not me, I never tell you nothing to make you worry."

"Then I reckon Our Lady must have told me, but what I want you to do is draw a warm bath for her while I explain the curse to her and then I want you to go to a store that has that package of gauze that is used to cope with it."

"Don't worry, I will, Miss Ella."

When Susie had left the bedroom, Aunt Ella drew a long breath.

"Dear child, this thing, the curse, without it the world would not continue and personally I think that would be a blessing instead of a curse. But we can discuss that later. What you do now is go and take a warm bath while Susie fetches the gauze, the, the—gauze. . . ."

The morphine drew her comfortably back into sleep and, hearing the water running in the bathroom, gently, soothingly, slowly, Rosemary moved that way.

When Susie returned with the gauze rolled in blue paper, she helped Rosemary to insert it, performing this help so discreetly that Rosemary didn't suffer too much embarrassment from it. Then she led Rosemary into that downstairs bedroom once occupied by Cornelius Dunphy. There was lovely fresh linen on the four-poster and four large snowy pillows. But what Rosemary most noticed in the room was that a rocker had been set beside the bed, in just the position, at the same angle, of the rocker in Aunt Ella's bedroom, the one reserved for the nightly visits of Our Lady.

Susie closed the shutters more firmly.

"Now, child, get into bed and I'll be back in a minute with a glass of warm milk and one of your Aunt Ella's tablets."

And it was not until Susie's departing footsteps faded from hearing that Rosemary knew what had happened to her. Aunt Ella had taken her captive. For a moment she thought of resisting. Then one of those jet planes flew over the house and when Susie came back with the milk and the tablet, Rosemary said: "A thunderstorm is coming."

"Yes, child, but don't you worry about it, it'll pass over soon, it's already passing over. Now wash down your tablet with this warm milk and don't be surprised if that Lady who visits your Aunt comes in here to set a while with you in this rocker your Aunt Ella had me put by the bed."

She tucked Rosemary into the bed and padded to the door very quietly. As she opened it she smiled at the captive maiden and said, "Miss Ella will expect you to stay for supper when you wake up, and, honey, I don't think she'd mind you staying on here for good."

November 1973

Oriflamme

Oriflamme

Immediately on waking that morning she felt the gravity of flesh which had virtually pinned her to her bed for weeks now mysteriously lifted away from her during the night. Some heavy sheath of air had unwound from her and had been replaced by atmosphere of an impalpable and electric kind. It could be the weather, changing from sullen to brilliant. All articles of glass in the room were pulsating with that brilliance as her body was with a renewed vitality.

Thoughtlessly she stretched her hand to the bedside phone, wanting to speak to someone: then the voices of the few people she knew rang dissonantly in her ears: there was not one voice among the babble of voices that she wanted to separate from the others, no, this morning's lightness couldn't be trusted to them. Which of them would be likely to say to her, Yes, I know what you mean, I understand what you're saying. The air is different this morning.

For there was a conspiracy of dullness in the world, a universal plan to shut out the resurgences of spirit which might interfere with clockwork. Better to keep your elevation unseen until it is higher than strangers' hands can reach to pull you down to their level.

She put the telephone down and sat on the edge of her bed. The little unsteadiness she felt in rising was not due to weakness but to this astonishing lack of gravity. Now here was a peculiar thing. Until this moment she had not understood the

93

meaning of her illness. It was all the same thing, sickness and fatigue and all attritions of the body and spirit, it all came from the natural anarchy of a heart that was compelled to wear uniform.

She went to her closet. It was full of discreetly colored and fashioned garments which all appeared the same style and shade and appeared to be designed for camouflage, for protective concealment, of that anarchy of the heart. She had lived up till now a subterranean existence, not only because she had employment in the economy basement of Famous-Barr, under the forbidding scrutiny of Mr. Mason and countless strangers who pinned her to the counter as illness had lately pinned her to the bed, but because she had not trusted the whisper in her that said, The truth has not yet been spoken!

Could she speak it?

There is speech and there are verbal symbols. The telephone had warned her against the first, but as she looked at the closet with its garments for winter, so appropriately descended from the backs of sheep, it occurred to her that revolution begins in putting on bright colors.

She left the closet and returned to the wardrobe trunk where lighter clothes were preserved for lighter seasons. She tore it open, breathing heavily with excitement. Disappointment was there also. The clothes smelt of camphor and none of them had a really challenging air.

She slammed the closet door shut, having snatched from it the first dress that came to her reach.

Obviously it was necessary to get hold of something new. . . .

She tore off her nightgown and stood shivering in front of the chilly closet mirror. How thin she was! No wonder she never looked really well in clothes. They could not express the mysterious delicacy of her body. It was white but not white. It was blue spilled delicately over white. And there were glints of silver and rose. Nobody knew about that. Only one person had ever seemed to suspect it. The high school dance in

Grenada, Mississippi. That red-faced boy who beat the kettle-drum so loudly and not in tempo and his virtuosity with the percussion had made Miss Fitzgerald so mad she had dragged him off the platform and slapped him and he had grinned and started dancing alone. She herself had then edged out a little from the corner she sat in, watching the couples dance. She was shy and had not been well lately. He had spun over to where she was standing and had wordlessly seized her and spun her with him around the yellow gymnasium and though she had started coughing and tasted the hot, metallic flavor of blood in her mouth, he had not let her go: not till they had gone clear around the room to the Blue Danube and had come to the festooned entrance. Then he had taken her arm and led her out. She tried to conceal the red stain on the hand that she had coughed into as soon as he had released her. But it was dark in the hall, nearly dark, and the two or three out there were grinning toward the brilliant entrance of the gymnasium.

Still not speaking he jerked her into another door. In there it was all dark completely and smelt of sweaty clothes. They banged against something that rang out like an ugly, toneless bell, the metal door of a locker. He backed her against it and pinioned her there while his hands explored her body. It was thrilling and shameful. Thrilling then and shameful afterward. Guy was the red boy's name. He had dropped out of school a week or two after this and had disappeared from Grenada. He was not heard of again until the following year when it became known that he had met with an accident on a freight train somewhere in the West. Had lost both legs. And later it became known that he was dead and that his widowed mother had said she was glad of it because he had broken her heart with his vagrant existence. . . .

Thinking of him she had always thought of those beautiful paper lanterns and crepe-paper ribbons that hung defeated in the yellow gymnasium. . . .

But that was so long ago now!

Outside!

It was indeed a new season if not a new world. The air had been given those shots which the doctor suggested. The blue was not only vivid but energetic. And there was white, too, the sort of white that her hidden body was made of. A mass of bonny white cloud stood over the Moolah Temple. It suddenly made up its mind and started moving. It moved now over the Langan & Taylor Storage. A nude young bather it was. An innocent white sky-lounger had taken off clothes and become a body that floats. And I shall, too. Or am already floating. Floating. The power of anarchy moves me. I have both legs. No accident has deprived me of forward motion. If chance is blind, it is still not set against me. And so I move. Past Langan & Taylor Storage and Hartwig's Beauty Salon. Past the doctor's suggestion, Go slowly and you'll go far. I am looking for something. But that means hesitation and I can't wait. He didn't and lost his legs. I still have mine and they're bearing me forward. I want, and will have, the banner that he let go of. The first that I see. Desire is. Wearing apparel. See and have on, that quickly. The white sky-lounger, capricious runner in heaven, has dropped a red dress somewhere. For me to put on and become her eternal sister. Oh, where? Not far off, Anna! The window is blazing with it already. Across the avenue, yes! In Paris Designs! The window is blazing with it. Correct as a go sign. Grab it!

She couldn't speak for a minute, her throat was too full of breathlessness—or breath.

I want that dress, she panted, the red one displayed in the window!

Very well, miss.

I haven't much time, please hurry!

I'm doing my best. It's a little bit difficult getting things out of the window.

Then let me do it!

That won't be necessary, the woman said coldly.

She now had the flag and was gingerly folding it up.

Her hands were gray. They were alien to the fabric as mice to roses. Their touch would wither it, dampen it, smother its flame.

Anna snatched the silk from her.

Don't wrap it up, madam! I want to put it on now!

The woman fell back as if cold water had drenched her.

But this is red silk, a dress for the evening, miss!

I realize that but I want to put it on now! Where is your dressing room?

Here, but—

Anna swept by her and plunged into the dim closet. The dress was all wine and roses flung onto her body.

Take by surprise and the world gives up resistance.

She paid the woman.

The blowing street took part in her celebration. She moved, she moved, in a glorious banner wrapped, the red part of a flag!

It flashed, it flashed. It billowed against her fingers. Her body surged forward. A capital ship with cannon. Boom. On the far horizon. Boom. White smoke is holy. Nobody understands it. It goes on, on, without the world's understanding. Red is holy. Nobody understands it. It goes on, on, without the world's understanding. Blue is holy. Blue goes on without the world's understanding. Flags are holy but nobody understands them. Flags go on without the world's understanding. Boom. Goes on without the world's understanding. The heart can't wait. Revolts without understanding. Boom. Goes on. Without the world's understanding. . . .

The red silk raised and lowered beneath her with power, the effortless power of wings that bore her forward. Into the brilliant new morning. No plan. No waiting. She moved without

97

a direction. Direction was unimportant. The world was lost. She felt it slipping behind her, a long way back. There was only Mr. Mason still in view. But even he was beginning to fall back now. Could not keep up his paunchy satyr pursuit. When young he could run. That season he first appeared at Famous-Barr, he was just out of college. He moved with a spring, was jaunty, inclined to jokes. The cloves on his breath were exciting. His manicured fingers were just removed from a fireplace. In locker-room blackness they might have been like Guy's, exploring, demanding, creating life in the blood. But the lights were never turned out in the bargain basement, and that one time they went to the Loew's State theater, his fingers had not adventured beyond her knee. The bus going home had been so everlasting. They ran out of talk and a self-conscious coldness developed. Before they reached the place where she got off, they were strangers. Her throat was so tight that she had distrusted her voice. At the door he had said, Well, this has been nice, Miss Kimball. And she, unable to open her mouth or her heart, had flung herself sobbing, not on the bed but on the floor—as soon as she heard his feet going down the steps. . . . The next day he had been jollier than ever. But with a difference. Why pretend? There is a failure with people. And that is why some people become so savage and tear at life and leave it in shreds and tatters. Because in gentleness there is failure so often. If you can't whisper, then it is wise to shout. Better to have it broken and violated but still in your clasp than never to have at all. In the end perhaps they understand more than you think and some remember and there is a fleshless reunion. . . .

He'd worn not well in the five years that had followed. When things don't change, their sameness becomes an accretion. That is why all society puts on flesh. Succumbs to the cubicles and begins to fill them. The bargain basement had put fat on Mr. Mason. The change boxes took his youth and gave him quarters. Some other girl now was employed at counter seven. Well, let her have it, the Pepperel and percale, and Mr.

Mason. And give her the scissors, give her the spool of tape. She would have assurance. A competent Miss she would be. She would cut through cloth with the long, sure stroke of an oarsman. As I cut now through the novel brilliance of morning! I, I am the red silk part of a flag! Let nobody stop me till I have—

She had become a little disoriented. Before her stood a gigantic equestrian statue. Her chin just reached the top of the granite pediment. There were the hooves on the level with her eyes. It looked as though the horse was about to step on her. Her eyes traveled upward to study the towering figure. All green it had turned with an ancient, mossy greenness. It bore a shield and elevated a sword. The look was fierce and compelling. Who was this stranger, this menacing giant on horseback? Her eyes descended to gaze at the inscription. *Saint Louis* it said. Ah, yes, the name of the city. No wonder she felt so breathless. She had climbed to the highest point in the park, and now if she turned to look in the other direction, all of the city named for this ruthless horseman would stretch underneath, to the east as far as the river. She would not turn. The city had never pleased her. The terrible horseman over the heads of people was image enough of what she felt in the city. Her hope had died in a basement of this city. Her faith had died in one of its smug churches. Her love had not survived a journey across it. She would not turn to face the sprawling city. Instead she would move across to that public fountain. No longer swiftly. What am I dragging behind me? Twenty-eight years and all those institutions. . . .

Now here is the fountain. But, no, it isn't a fountain. It is a shallow cement bowl for sparrows. But even the sparrows have found it a false invitation. The bowl is dry. It contains a few oak leaves disintegrating. And all this green. I wasn't prepared for green. The green has to be taken gently. Not swallowed but

99

sipped the way birds do water if bowls aren't dry. But all at once in a gulf of green too quickly! All men have known, adventurers and pilgrims, that green is the stuff that sweeps you down and under. Cannot be trusted, is eager to overwhelm you. A butterfly boat that a child lets go in the dusk is safer than I in the middle of this green breaking. Go slowly now. The earth is still horizontal. But awfully windy. There's too much sky to let go of and too much to keep. But friendlier than this avalanche of green. Now, where has she gone, that amiable young sky pilgrim, that innocent nude without any avoirdupois? Oh, yes, I see her. A long way off to the left. She has made good progress! And I? I've come to the—

No. Sit down on that bench over there till my breath comes back. This pain reminds me of school inoculations. . . .

Close to the one where the birds were disappointed, Anna herself was all at once a fountain. The foam of a scarlet ocean crossed her lips. Oh, oh. The ocean the butterfly boat is a voyager on. . . .

The green of leaves, the scarlet ocean of blood, together they wash and break on the deathless blue. It makes a flag—but nobody understands it. . . .

January 1944 (The month of my grandmother's death in St. Louis)

100

New Directions Paperbooks

Walter Abish, *Alphabetical Africa*. NDP375.
Minds Meet. NDP387.
Ilangô Adigal, *Shilappadikaram*. NDP162.
Alain, *The Gods*. NDP382.
G. Apollinaire, *Selected Writings*.† NDP310.
Djuna Barnes, *Nightwood*. NDP98.
Charles Baudelaire, *Flowers of Evil*.† NDP71.
Paris Spleen. NDP294.
Gottfried Benn, *Primal Vision*.† NDP322.
Eric Bentley, *Bernard Shaw*. NDP59.
Wolfgang Borchert, *The Man Outside*. NDP319.
Jorge Luis Borges, *Labyrinths*. NDP186.
Jean-François Bory, *Once Again*. NDP256.
Kay Boyle, *Thirty Stories*. NDP62.
E. Brock, *Invisibility Is The Art of Survival*.
NDP342.
Paroxisms. NDP385.
The Portraits & The Poses. NDP360.
Buddha, *The Dhammapada*. NDP188.
Frederick Busch, *Manual Labor*. NDP376.
Ernesto Cardenal, *In Cuba*. NDP377.
Hayden Carruth, *For You*. NDP298.
From Snow and Rock, from Chaos. NDP349.
Louis-Ferdinand Céline,
Death on the Installment Plan. NDP330.
Guignol's Band. NDP278.
Journey to the End of the Night. NDP84.
Blaise Cendrars, *Selected Writings*.† NDP203.
B-c. Chatterjee, *Krishnakanta's Will*. NDP120.
Jean Cocteau, *The Holy Terrors*. NDP212.
The Infernal Machine. NDP235.
M. Cohen, *Monday Rhetoric*. NDP352.
Cid Corman, *Livingdying*. NDP289.
Sun Rock Man. NDP318.
Gregory Corso, *Elegiac Feelings American*.
NDP299.
Happy Birthday of Death. NDP86.
Long Live Man. NDP127.
Edward Dahlberg, *Reader*. NDP246.
Because I Was Flesh. NDP227.
David Daiches, *Virginia Woolf*. NDP96.
Osamu Dazai, *The Setting Sun*. NDP258.
No Longer Human. NDP357.
Coleman Dowell, *Mrs. October Was Here*.
NDP368.
Robert Duncan, *Bending the Bow*. NDP255.
The Opening of the Field. NDP356.
Roots and Branches. NDP275.
Richard Eberhart, *Selected Poems*. NDP198.
Russell Edson. *The Falling Sickness*. NDP 389.
The Very Thing That Happens. NDP137.
Paul Eluard, *Uninterrupted Poetry*. NDP392.
Wm. Empson, *7 Types of Ambiguity*. NDP204.
Some Versions of Pastoral. NDP92.
Wm. Everson, *Man-Fate*. NDP369.
The Residual Years. NDP263.
Lawrence Ferlinghetti, *Her*. NDP88.
Back Roads to Far Places. NDP312.
A Coney Island of the Mind. NDP74.
The Mexican Night. NDP300.
Open Eye, Open Heart. NDP361.
Routines. NDP187.
The Secret Meaning of Things. NDP268.
Starting from San Francisco. NDP 220.
Tyrannus Nix?. NDP288.
Ronald Firbank, *Two Novels*. NDP128.
Dudley Fitts,
Poems from the Greek Anthology. NDP60.
F. Scott Fitzgerald, *The Crack-up*. NDP54.
Robert Fitzgerald, *Spring Shade: Poems
1931-1970*. NDP311.
Gustave Flaubert.
Bouvard and Pécuchet. NDP328.
The Dictionary of Accepted Ideas. NDP230.
M. K. Gandhi, *Gandhi on Non-Violence*.
(ed. Thomas Merton) NDP197.
André Gide, *Dostoevsky*. NDP100.
Goethe, *Faust*, Part I.
(MacIntyre translation) NDP70.
Albert J. Guerard, *Thomas Hardy*. NDP185.

Guillevic, *Selected Poems*.† NDP279.
Henry Hatfield, *Goethe*. NDP136.
Thomas Mann. (Revised Edition) NDP101.
John Hawkes, *The Beetle Leg*. NDP239.
The Blood Oranges. NDP338.
The Cannibal. NDP123.
Death, Sleep & The Traveler. NDP393.
The Innocent Party. NDP238.
The Lime Twig. NDP95.
Lunar Landscapes. NDP274.
Second Skin. NDP146.
A. Hayes, *A Wreath of Christmas Poems*.
NDP347.
H.D., *Helen in Egypt*. NDP380
Hermetic Definition NDP343.
Trilogy. NDP362.
Robert E. Helbling, *Heinrich von Kleist*, NDP390.
Hermann Hesse, *Siddhartha*. NDP65.
Christopher Isherwood, *The Berlin Stories*.
NDP134.
Gustav Janouch,
Conversations With Kafka. NDP313.
Alfred Jarry, *Ubu Roi*, NDP105.
Robinson Jeffers, *Cawdor and Medea*. NDP293.
James Joyce, *Stephen Hero*. NDP133.
James Joyce/Finnegans Wake. NDP331.
Franz Kafka, *Amerika*. NDP117.
Bob Kaufman,
Solitudes Crowded with Loneliness. NDP199.
Hugh Kenner, *Wyndham Lewis*. NDP167.
Kenyon Critics, *Gerard Manley Hopkins*.
NDP355.
P. Lal, *Great Sanskrit Plays*. NDP142.
Tommaso Landolfi,
Gogol's Wife and Other Stories. NDP155.
Lautréamont, *Maldoror*. NDP207.
Denise Levertov, *Footprints*. NDP344.
The Jacob's Ladder. NDP112.
O Taste and See. NDP149.
The Poet in the World. NDP363.
Relearning the Alphabet. NDP290.
The Sorrow Dance. NDP222.
To Stay Alive. NDP325.
With Eyes at the Back of Our Heads.
NDP229.
Harry Levin, *James Joyce*. NDP87.
García Lorca, *Five Plays*. NDP232.
Selected Poems.† NDP114.
Three Tragedies. NDP52.
Michael McClure, *September Blackberries*.
NDP370.
Carson McCullers, *The Member of the
Wedding*. (Playscript) NDP153.
Thomas Merton, *Cables to the Ace*. NDP252.
Asian Journal. NDP394.
Emblems of a Season of Fury. NDP140.
Gandhi on Non-Violence. NDP197.
The Geography of Lograire. NDP283.
New Seeds of Contemplation. NDP337.
Raids on the Unspeakable. NDP213.
Selected Poems. NDP85.
The Way of Chuang Tzu. NDP276.
The Wisdom of the Desert. NDP295.
Zen and the Birds of Appetite. NDP261.
Henri Michaux, *Selected Writings*.† NDP264.
Henry Miller, *The Air-Conditioned Nightmare*.
NDP302.
*Big Sur & The Oranges of Hieronymus
Bosch*. NDP161.
The Books in My Life. NDP280.
The Colossus of Maroussi. NDP75.
The Cosmological Eye. NDP109.
Henry Miller on Writing. NDP151.
The Henry Miller Reader. NDP269.
Remember to Remember. NDP111.
The Smile at the Foot of the Ladder. NDP386.
Stand Still Like the Hummingbird. NDP236.
The Time of the Assassins. NDP115.
The Wisdom of the Heart. NDP94.
Y. Mishima, *Confessions of a Mask*. NDP253.
Death in Midsummer. NDP215.
Eugenio Montale, *Selected Poems*.† NDP193.

Complete descriptive catalog available free on request from
New Directions, 333 Sixth Avenue, New York 10014.   † Bilingual